Teatime

CHRIS BREVA

Teatime

A collection of short stories and other writings

ReadersMagnet, LLC

Teatime: A Collection of Short Stories and Other Writings

Published in the United States of America
ISBN Paperback: 978-1-954371-86-6
ISBN Hardback: 978-1-955603-36-2
ISBN eBook: 978-1-954371-87-3

All Bible citations are from the King James Version.

ReadersMagnet, LLC
10620 Treena Street, Suite 230 | San Diego, California, 92131 USA
1.619.354.2643 | www.readersmagnet.com

Cover design by Kent Gabutin
Interior design by Renalie Malinao

Contents

Comedy

Christmas Stories

Psychic Encounter / Horror

Fantasy and Science Fiction

Westerns

Essays

True Stories

Christian Essays

Poetry

Oriental Poetry

COMEDY

Cat-in-Mouth Disease

My dad was a raging alcoholic in my younger years. Fortunately, he died sober. He passed on February 10, 2015. During his drinking days he was usually very cruel. However, there were times when he was outright comedic. For example, we heard him gasping one evening. Being concerned we went to check on him. What we found was a picture I will never forget! He was wearing one of Mom's nightgowns. He later explained that it was a gift and he wanted to surprise Mom by modeling it for her. He succeeded!

To make matters even funnier, he had picked up a kitten and stuck its head in his mouth! So, there he was dressed in Mom's nightgown with a kitten sticking out of his mouth. He signaled for help with the kitten but got none until a picture was taken. Do not worry. The kitten was unharmed. Dad on the other was not. You see the kitten got anxious and went ballistic! It scratched his face to pieces before it was released. (We have some great pics of that as well.)

He did not want to explain that to the doctor! So, he let his face heal on its own. He bore scars until the day he died. When anybody asked about the scars, he would tell them they were from Cat in Mouth Disease!

Harry, the Sheriff, and the Lemons

Nobody knew what was wrong with Angry Harry. The truth never came out. However, the sheriff caught him down on Seven Bridges Road throwing lemons at an old-vacant house. The story was that the sheriff really did not want to arrest Angry Harry. He simply wanted Angry Harry to quit throwing lemons at the vacant house. Angry Harry refused to do so however, and began throwing lemons at the sheriff as well!

"What's gotten into you Harry?" asked the sheriff as the lemons kept pelting the cruiser. "I know you're a little screwy. You always have been. This just is not like you though. Now cease throwing lemons at my cruiser or the vacant house or I will be forced to place you under arrest."

"You can arrest me if you want sheriff, but I own that vacant house and I own the lemons. So, it seems to me I can do whatever I want with either one."

"You are right Angry Harry. If you own the house, it is yours to destroy if you want to destroy it. However, you cannot be throwing lemons at my cruiser or I because you own neither. Now why don't you just simmer down and tell me what is going on?"

"Did it occur to you that perhaps I just want to stand here on Seven Bridges Road and throw lemons at a vacant house?" Angry Harry asked.

"No it hadn't," replied the sheriff. "I'll tell you what though. Stop throwing lemons at my cruiser and I will join you."

After that nobody could figure out why Angry Harry and the sheriff were sighted on Seven Bridges Road throwing lemons at Angry Harry's vacant house!

Strange Fruit Salad

I was in the Spend – It – All supermarket one day doing my grocery shopping. Being a glutton for punishment I always went there to shop. I loved their extortionist prices and their poor-quality products. My family hated them but that was alright with me. I did not really like my family anyway. I mean I had to love them. They were family but I did not like them.

I was hungry for some citrus products, so I went to the fruit section to see what was available. Lo and behold, the fruits they had were more than merely exotic. They were downright strange! Why they had such oddities as red bananas, orange grapes, silver cherries, black apples, maroon pineapples, and purple oranges. I could not resist giving them all a try. In fact, I was going to use them to make the strangest fruit salad my family had ever eaten. So, I bought several containers of each and took them home. When I arrived, I asked my dead-beat son to carry the groceries in. "Oh Mom," he complained. "I'm playing Attack of the Idiots on my computer."

"I really don't care what you're doing," his nearly as useless father replied. "You get out there and help your mother carry those groceries in, so I don't have to, you know me and my back!"

"Yes Dad," Milbourne replied. "We know you scraped it on the table two months ago and you're probably going to cry yourself to death over it. I will go carry the groceries in. I would not want you to strain your scratches. They may start bleeding!"

Satisfied that I may actually get a little cooperation from Milbourne, I went to the kitchen to prepare the pantry. Soon the groceries were all carried in, thanks in part to Milbourne carrying one bag and my carrying the remaining bags. Once they were in the kitchen, I began putting them away as the dopey twins stood watching me. "Oh," I told them "I've got a special treat in store for you both. I am calling it strange fruit salad. Wait until you see the ingredients!"

"Anything you cook is strange," said my husband Terry. "So, whatever you have in store, I am sure we do not want!"

"Thank you for the vote of confidence and your always loving support," I retorted. "I think you'll really like this though. If you do, I'll make more of it."

What he didn't know was that I'd make more of it whether he liked it or not. He could either eat it or start losing his excessive abdomen. I really didn't care which.

"Here are the ingredients," I said as I began pulling the strange fruit out of the bag.

"It will have purple oranges, white pears, red bananas, silver cherries, orange grapes, black apples, maroon pineapple, and yellow watermelon. Doesn't that sound delicious?"

"I have to give you credit," Terry replied, "because you were right about one thing. It certainly is strange. Strange enough that Milbourne can have my serving!"

"Touché Dad," Milbourne replied. "I was going to give you mine and go eat the dog food."

"Come on you two," I said. "How do you know you are going to hate it before you even try it?"

"Mom," Milbourne said. "I can give you two very good reasons why I'm not going to try it. They're fear and common sense."

"Well I always knew you had plenty of fear in you," Terry told him. "The common sense is a new one on me though!"

"Would you like to step outside Old Man," Milbourne asked his dad teasingly. "I think I could whip you in a fair fight."

"The only way a fight between us would be fair is if I had two broken legs, a broken back, and was either blind or blindfolded," Terry replied.

"Well you two scram while I start dinner," I told my worthless loved ones.

It did not take me long to have dinner prepared. I cut up the fruit and put it in the biggest bowl I had. When the last of it was in the bowl, I stirred it all together. Then I called the two knuckleheads to come to dinner. I served them each a huge bowl of my strange fruit salad. "Where did Shaggy hide his dog food bowl?" Terry asked. "I'll split it with you son!"

Confused Animals

I can tell you a true story about a cat raised with a litter of pups. We lived on a large farm and had all sorts of animals. Many of the animals we had were livestock and many other pets. Two of the animals we had were a dog who was a bitch and a female cat. The bitch and the cat both got pregnant and I do not recall the timing of which was which. However, the bitch was nursing at the same time the female cat would have been nursing. The female cat only had three kittens, two of which did not make it. She left the third to go out for some reason. While she was out, she was run over by a car and got killed. We were left with a kitten that we had no idea what to do with. Somebody suggested putting it down but that was not the answer. Somebody else suggested feeding it with an eyedropper but we could not afford milk for ourselves a lot of times. Finally, the suggestion was made to let the female dog nurse it. Everybody shrugged and thought, "What the heck?"

So the kitten was placed among the puppies and the bitch began raising it as if it were her pup! The kitten and the puppies bonded and became a family. It was comical to watch the much bigger puppies play with the kitten, but they were very gentle as if just assuming it was the runt of the litter! They never once got rough with it and taught it to fight like a dog! It probably would have been better off if it had learned to fight like a cat because any cat can handle even a St. Bernard with ease.

This motley crew played together for months and the cat did pick up a few of the dog behaviors. It tried to play fetch but could not bite onto either a ball or a stick because its mouth simply was not that big. Instead, it simply played with it. One thing it did do that most cats do not is sit on its behind like a dog. The typical behavior of a cat is to simply lie down. So, the cat acted like a dog.

A few years later somebody dumped a puppy near our house. It was obvious that the pup was at best two weeks old, probably younger and had no chance of survival without a mother. However, we had no nursing dogs. What we did have was a cat who had lost three of her litter. (It was a different cat.) So, we remembered the situation with the cat, who was still with us even then, and we placed the puppy with the mother cat. She adopted it hesitantly but since it was practically a newborn whose eyes were not even open, she took it in. As the puppy developed, he acted like a cat. He would swat at his opponents rather than bite them. What was funniest was to watch him hunch his back up before he attacked!

Three Wishes

There was once a fisherman named Bob Foley. He lived on a river called White Water. His favorite past time was fishing. Bob always fished in the same place. He fished at a Locks and Dam on the White-Water River. The natives knew the place by Pier Seventeen. Unlike anybody else who ever fished at Pier Seventeen however, Bob was constantly turning up some new mysterious situation. It is very odd because it never happened to anybody else. It was always poor old Bob.

Bob thought about giving up fishing, but he just could not bring himself to do so. He enjoyed fishing when strange things did not happen. Of course, strange things consistently happened to him. Each time, he would talk himself into trying it one more time. He was like a child who kept getting burned on a hot stove, but never learned to quit touching the stove. This Saturday morning was no different. It was a hot day in July and Bob talked himself into going fishing. He was convinced that surely this time nothing bad would happen to him. So, he loaded up his pole, his tackle, and his bait and went down to Pier Seventeen. He had a new lure he was just dying to try out. The man at the bait shop had told him the lure would practically hunt down the largest bass in the water and insert itself into the bass' mouth. Well, he did not quite believe that, but it made the lure look mighty appealing to him. So, he secured it to the line and cast it into the water. The lure had no more than hit the water when lo and behold, he snagged a whopper! He fought with the bass for a good ten minutes and finally got it reeled in. He went to take it off the hook when the strangest thing happened. The bass spoke to him! "Bob," it said. "Bob please let me go. Please do not eat me. I am a magic bass and if you let me go, I will grant you three wishes."

Well Bob didn't believe in magic, but he couldn't bring himself to eat a talking fish, so he let the bass go. A few minutes later he decided to go to his truck and look for a missing tackle box. He had a little bit of obsessive-compulsive disorder going on. He had already looked in the bed of the truck for the missing tackle box three times, so he knew it was not there. His obsessive-compulsive disorder made him go look again. Still, it was not there. "I wish I could find that tackle box," he said.

He went to turn around to go back to the river and tripped over something. He looked down and it was his missing tackle box. Suddenly, he heard the bass say, "That's wish number one Bob. I would be careful. You have two wishes remaining."

He walked back down to the river and prepared to cast his line in again. A bead of sweat ran down his brow and got in his eye. Without thinking he said, "I wish it would cool down a little bit. Suddenly, a cool breeze began to blow. The bass said, "That is wish number two Bob. You only have one wish left. Use it wisely."

Bob sat and carefully considered his situation. There were so many things his wife and he needed. A new house would be nice. A Swiss bank account with nine zeroes would be nice as well. There were just so many things. He heard himself say, "I wish I could make up my mind!"

Warum hast Du nicht nein gesagt

Jimmy and his brother Bob were standing on the bank of the river fishing on a hot summer day. As is often the case when it is hot, the fish were not biting at all. Bob sat down on his lounge chair and sat back so he could see his pole if he needed to but felt certain it was a moot point. Both Jimmy and he had stakes driven into the ground, the tops of which were angled into a V shape. The idea was that if a large fish took the bait and tugged hard on the poles, the rods would stop their fishing poles from being dragged into the river and lost forever. Just as Bob made himself comfortable, his pole bent nearly double and the back of it jumped into the air as a large fish struggled with the hook on the end of the line. Bob grabbed the pole and stood up to begin the struggle of reeling the fish in. Jimmy stood beside him, coaching him and encouraging him not to pull too hard or he may break the line. It was quite a struggle, but after a few minutes Bob pulled the biggest largemouth bass he had ever seen from the river.

He reached up and got a high five from Jimmy and prepared to take the big fish off the hook. Like many rivers, the river he was fishing in was so polluted that he had no intention of keeping anything he caught. He was merely fishing to be fishing. Suddenly however the strangest event took place. The fish spoke to him! "Kind prince," the bass said, "if you will permit me to go free, I will grant you any wish you make."

After Bob got his heart started again from the shock of a talking fish he said, "Yeah right! You're supposed to be magic fish but didn't have the power to know the worm was actually bait. You also do not have the power to know that I never had any intentions of keeping you to begin with. However, now that I know you are a talking fish; I am going to keep you because you are very valuable. I'll be rich and famous."

"I don't have ESP," the bass said, "and you won't be rich because I won't talk regardless of what you do to me. You will look like a fool. If you let me go through, I will see to it that you have huge amounts of money and that your name makes the nightly news."

"Make it 10 million dollars and you've got a deal," Bob said.

"Ten million it is," said the bass. "It's in your bank account now by wire transfer."

"Let me confirm it," Bob said.

"Well hurry up," the bass said. "This tank is awfully small. And throw some bait in here. I'm hungry!"

Bob called the bank and inquired about his account balance. When the clerk told him he had ten million dollars spread out over several accounts, he was elated. He told them he would be in shortly to make a withdrawal. Then, he thanked the bass and let it go. Jimmy and he went to the bank. Bob identified himself to the cashier. "We've been expecting you Mr. Rossellini," a voice behind him said. "I'm Special Agent Forbes, US Secret Service, this is my partner Special Agent in Charge, Cliff Fielding. You sir are under arrest for embezzlement."

"Embezzlement!" Bob exclaimed. "What am I supposed to have embezzled?"

"Your computer shows that you hacked into a social security fund and embezzled ten million dollars."

"***Warum hast Du nicht nein gesagt***," said Jimmy. ***"Why didn't you say no?"***

Later that night after he had been booked by the police and put in jail, Bob was watching television. The news came on and to his surprise, he was the headline story for the national news. He remembered that the fish had told him he would be on the news. "***Warum hast Du nicht nein gesagt,***" Bob said to himself. "***Warum hast Du nicht nein gesagt.***"

CHRISTMAS STORIES

Rolling Thunder

Rolling Thunder was a horse that lived in a faraway land called Anthromorphia. Each year he would stand in the pasture grazing and awaiting the coming of Christmas. It was his hope that he would get to have a talk with Santa Claus after the Anthromorphia Christmas parade this year. He knew exactly what he would ask the jolly old elf for. He pranced as he stood in line with his girlfriend waiting to see Santa.

"Are you standing here thinking about asking Santa Claus for something totally outrageous?" asked Queen Bee, his favorite young filly.

"Yes," he answered, despite knowing that she thought he was crazy. "I sure do hope Santa gives me what I want this year. I have something very special I want to ask him for."

"What do you want him to bring you," the pretty young Appaloosa filly asked him.

"I don't want him to bring me anything," Rolling Thunder answered. "I want him to grant me a favor."

"What favor will you ask of him then?" Queen Bee asked.

"I'd ask him to grant me the ability to fly and allow me to lead his sleigh team one year. If I could not lead it, at least make me part of it."

"That's what I love about you Thunder," Queen Bee answered. "You never quit dreaming and when you dream, you do it with gusto."

"Pulling a sleigh isn't so much a dream for a horse," Thunder answered. "You and I are both more than capable of pulling a sleigh."

"That's very true," she replied, fearing she may have hurt his feelings. "But we're not talking about a sleigh that slides along through the woods."

After what seemed an eternity, the line was gone, and it was Rolling Thunder's turn to talk to Santa Claus. He felt very nervous considering what he was going to ask but he put on a brave face and went forward.

"What can I do for you today Thunder?" asked Santa.

"It's not so much what you can do for me Santa," Thunder replied. "It's more about what I want to do for you. You see I am a horse. I am very powerful, and I can run like the wind. Therefore, I wanted to see if it may be possible for me to join your team this year and help pull your sleigh?"

"Well I don't know Thunder," Santa replied. "To be totally honest with you, I've never considered using a horse as a member of my sleigh team. However, I suspect my reindeer may be a bit intimidated by your presence. I know you've really got your heart set on helping me out though, so I'll give it a great deal of thought."

"Okay Santa," Thunder replied.

As they were speaking, a technician from the parade approached them. "Santa?" the technician asked. "I know that you normally use reindeer but we're having a problem with your sleigh. It came off the truck we had it on, and it is stuck in a snowbank. It is much too heavy for us to move. Can we borrow your horse team and pull it out?"

"Well it's not my decision to make," said Santa. "It would be up to the horses. However, I think I can speak for one when I say that I am sure you can find a volunteer or two."

Once Rolling Thunder and Queen Bee had successfully pulled Santa's sleigh out of the embankment of snow, he allowed them to pull him up the street and out of sight of everybody else. "Are you two ready?" Santa asked. "Here we go!"

Suddenly, Thunder felt his hooves leave the ground as he galloped into the air. He was doing it! He was pulling Santa's sleigh through the sky!

The First Noel

I was attending church services one Christmas eve. There was a young man sitting there dressed in clothing that appeared to be customary of Israeli first century clothing. So, this got my attention. I thought perhaps the church had planned a Christmas play and I was not aware of it. I approached the boy and asked him if I could sit with him.

"Yes you may," he answered. "May I ask what your name is?"

"I'm Ariel," I answered. "I attend church here. I do not recall seeing you around here before though. Since you are here, perhaps you can tell me if Pastor Wolfe planned and rehearsed a Christmas play with you children without our knowledge. I ask because you look like you'd be playing the role of one of the shepherds who was in the field the night the angels announced the birth of the Savior."

"I look like one of the shepherds because I am one of the shepherds," the boy replied, making me think he had blown a fuse. "My name is Eli, son of Jacob, son of Nathaniel, son of Enoch, son of Seth, son of Joseph..."

"Shhh," I told him, "it will be okay."

"You should have been there," the boy said. "We were out in the grazing land about a day's walk from Bethlehem. It was a warm evening, and the stars were shining so bright it looked like you could reach up and pluck them right out of the sky. There was a new star in the sky that night. It was by far brighter than any of the others. The funny thing is that the new star disappeared after some time and was never seen again. Our sheep were resting, and all was well."

I wanted to tell the child to be quiet and allow me to listen to the service instead of his wild tales. However, the way he told the story had me sitting on the edge of my seat! As I glanced around, I noticed that everybody else, including the preacher, had stopped what they were doing and were listening to the boy tell his story.

"All of a sudden," the boy said, "the entire sky lit up. It was very frightening to us because we had never seen such a thing. A loud voice spoke to us and said *'Do not fear. We have come to bring you tidings of hope and good cheer. Unto you this night, in the city of David is born a Savior who shall be named Christ.'*

"Then there was the most beautiful singing anybody has ever heard. The singing was more beautiful than ten thousand harps, lyres, and stringed instruments. Far more beautiful even than the musicians David put in the tabernacle. The other shepherds and I stared at the sight in silence not knowing what to say. The angels kept singing and we joined them. They sang *"Holy, holy, holy, worthy is he has come in the name of the Lord."*

Everybody in the church had gathered around the boy now. Each of us wanted to ask him questions but nobody wanted to interrupt his story. It seemed incredible to believe that this child had witnessed the first noel, yet the way he told the story seemed like an actual firsthand account, not like something he had learned.

"The singing went on for some minutes and then stopped," the boy said. "The other shepherds and I discussed what it meant. Could this be the birth of the Promised One? We did not know. One thing we were certain of though. We were certain we had just been visited by messengers of God. It is an experience we never forgot. We made a promise among ourselves that we would never tell anybody what we saw that night. We knew however that we were visited by angels."

The little boy didn't say another word. I prepared to ask him the first of the many questions circulating in my head when he placed his fingers across his lips signaling me to be quiet. Then he disappeared as if he were never there.

Piney, The Christmas Tree

Piney stood tall and proud in the thicket as people scurried all around searching for that perfect Christmas tree. There were a variety of evergreens available on the Christmas tree farm. The owner George Marlett had planted everything from a blue spruce thicket to a white pine thicket. Piney was a Canaan Fir. He stood just over 7 feet tall and was about ten feet in diameter. His leaves or needles were dark green in color as compared to the red cedar, which had needles with a pinkish hue in the winter months. Yes! Piney would make an excellent Christmas tree. The problem was that most of the other trees in his thicket would also make excellent Christmas trees. It was the dream of any evergreen tree to become a Christmas tree. Doing so was an honor greater than any other.

Piney watched as tree after tree left the thicket and went to its new home. Piney however was not selected. He knew that this would be the last Christmas for which he would have the opportunity to be a Christmas tree. In another year, he would be much too big. Today was the last day as well. Although Christmas was still two weeks away, Mr. Marlett had been in business long enough that he really did not need the money, so he was closing well before Christmas. Thus, Piney knew that if he were not selected today, he would miss his opportunity to be a Christmas tree.

Group after group of people came into the thicket to get the popular Canaan firs. With each tree that was taken, Piney's hopes would both wax and wane. He became excited because each tree taken was one less left to choose from. On the other hand, he knew time was running out. If he were not selected soon, he would not be selected at all.

Soon, Marlett closed the farm for the season and Piney was still there. Piney's heart was broken because he had so wanted to be a Christmas tree. He could just see himself standing tall in somebody's house with an angel or star perched in his highest branches, ornate bulbs of gold, silver, red, blue, and green hanging from his branches, garland swirled everywhere on him, and electric lights blinking on and off. Oh, what a tree he would have made! Now it was all merely a pipe dream because the farm was closed. In fact, the sun had now set in the west. It was pitch dark. Piney could not see six inches in front of his eyes. Piney wanted to cry because he had not been selected. Now all hope was gone. Then he heard something. It was faint at first, but it became louder and louder. It was George Marlett's voice!

"I normally wouldn't do this," Marlett said, "however because it's you I'm willing to make an exception."

"I understand," the other gentleman answered, "and I appreciate you being so thoughtful and considerate."

"Well, maybe you'll be considerate of me in return one day," Marlett ventured.

"Soon," the voice responded, "very soon."

Piney thought he recognized the voice of the other gentleman but he couldn't quite remember who it was. Both men were carrying flashlights, which blinded Piney just as much as the darkness had earlier. "I'll take this one," the gentleman's voice said as he held one of Piney's limbs. "I think the Mrs. will like it."

Soon Piney was dug up as the gentleman requested, his roots and the earth around them wrapped in a rag, and he was loaded into what felt like a truck or something. Then the gentleman got into the vehicle and spoke. "Let's go Rudolph!"

Santa-Napped

"Who's there?" Santa asked, feeling slightly uneasy as a shadowy figure lurked in his quarters. "Is that you Mama?"

The figure did not say a word. Instead, it approached his bed and stood over him. "I don't know who you are," Santa said. "But you aren't supposed to..."

His words trailed off as a rag was forced over his nose and he succumbed to the chloroform. The kidnapper managed to slip away unnoticed, taking Santa from his North Pole home.

When Santa came to, he looked around at his surroundings. He quickly surmised that he was in a cage that even his magic could not unlock. He was also bound with garland, which to him was as strong as the toughest steel. "Where am I?" he demanded.

"You're safe for now," the kidnapper answered.

"Grinch!" Santa growled. "I should have known you were behind this! You have been trying to stop Christmas for as long as I can remember. Well kidnapping me is not going to stop Christmas. My helpers will see to it that every good little child in the world gets the things they want on Christmas whether I am there or not!"

"I don't think they will," Grinch replied. "I've seen the way those bunch of bumbling fools act without you there. They wouldn't be able to dress themselves without your help."

"We'll see about that," Santa answered. "Don't you think that I've already considered the possibility that I may be incapacitated in some way and that I've made contingency plans? You cannot stop Christmas! Now, let me go! Perhaps, I can be persuaded to ask the Council of Magical Beings to have mercy on you this time. If not, my staff will rescue me and you will be in big trouble."

"I have no concern with the Council," Grinch replied. "Their rulings mean nothing to me anyway. Besides, nobody knows where you are or what became of you. I'm only keeping you safe while I decide how to dispose of you."

Mrs. Claus meanwhile went into Santa's sleeping quarters to take him a hot bowl of chicken soup. She knew he had been feeling a bit weary of late and hoped the soup would perk him up a little. When she found he was not there however, she at first thought he had gone to check on the progress of the elves. After all, it was only three days until he would make his annual trip and he would want to be sure everything was on schedule. So, she was going to dismiss his absence as normal until she saw his boots sitting beside his bed. She knew Santa well enough to know that he would not even go to the bathroom without his boots on. Something was drastically wrong.

"Alert the Elf rescue squad," Mrs. Claus told Jasmine, her helper elf. "Something drastic has happened to Santa. I am sure of it. He is not here, and his boots are still here. Santa doesn't go anyplace without his boots because his feet are much too tender."

The elf rescue squad arrived in moments and began scouring the room for signs of what may have become of Santa. One of the elves looked under Santa's bed and found the chloroform-soaked rag. "It's chloroform," he told Mrs. Claus and his partners. "It looks like Santa has been Santa-napped. Now we must figure out who did it and how to rescue Santa. Roderique, activate the homing beacon Santa had implanted in his tooth but set it on silent. We do not want the Santa-napper to hear it. Sergio, begin a database search of all of Santa's known enemies. Maybe we can eliminate the suspects that way."

"Santa has no enemies," Mrs. Claus stated. "Everybody loves him."

"We all have some enemies ma'am," Elf Rescue Squad leader Hernando stated. "Maybe Santa doesn't have many but I'm sure even he has made somebody angry. Now we just must figure out who he has made angry and why they would kidnap him."

"The why part is easy," Ferdinand the elf said. "The obvious reason anybody would kidnap Santa is to stop Christmas."

"Who would want to stop Christmas?" Hernando asked, "and why would they want to do so?"

"Grinch," they all replied in unison.

"Yes," said Hernando. "He has been trying to stop Christmas for eons! Where was his last known location? I know Santa had a team assigned to watch him closely, but he is as slick as a greased pig. He could easily have kidnapped Santa."

"The last time we knew he was still located on Grinch Mountain," Ferdinand replied. "With your permission I volunteer to lead a team to go there and if Santa's there, rescue him."

"Permission granted," Hernando stated. "When you arrive, scan the mountain and see how many magical creatures are there. The Grinch himself is a magical creature. If there are two magical beings there however, the second is likely Santa Claus. Use your invisibility powers to become invisible and rescue Santa. Grinch cannot penetrate your invisibility powers. He will never know what happened. If he did Santa-nap Santa Claus, arrest him. as well. Bring him back here to be tried by the Council of Magical Beings."

Ferdinand arrived at Grinch Mountain with a team of elves a few minutes later. He retrieved the scanner and set it to search. Sure enough, deep within the mountain, he read the presence of two magical beings. One had the known characteristics of Grinch and the other was undoubtedly Santa Claus. "Yes," Ferdinand told his team. "Santa is definitely here. From what I can read on the scanner, he is being held in cage that magic will not penetrate. He is also tied with garland which renders him helpless. Turn on your invisibility gear. Grinch will not be able to see you. Our orders are to rescue Santa and arrest Grinch. Alfred you take point."

Within a few seconds, the elves had traveled through hundreds of tons of dirt and stone to find themselves standing in the lair of the meanest and most horrible Christmas character of all time: Grinch! Without a sound, Ferdinand walked over to Santa's cell and slipped through the bars. His size made the bars easy to pass through. Once inside, he untied the garland restraining Santa. Alfred, during the meantime, unlocked the cell. They both knew that even if Santa was untied, his magic would be useless in the locked cell. Once the door was unlocked however, Santa could use his magic freely.

Two other elves who were also invisible came up behind Grinch. Without hesitation, they quickly subdued him by placing a pair of love cuffs on his wrists. Love overcame all barriers. As soon as the love cuffs were placed on Grinch's scrawny wrists however, an amazing thing happened. The stone cold, ice cold heart in Grinch's chest began to melt away and it was replaced with a loving heart.

"What have I done," Grinch cried. "I nearly stopped Christmas! Oh! How could I have ever been so evil? Santa, can you ever forgive me? If you will, I will make it up to you. In fact, if you will allow me to do so, I would like to ride along with you as you deliver the toys this year. Oh! To see the smiles on the faces of children!"

St. Nicholas's Vacation

St. Nicholas, otherwise known as Santa Claus, had just finished his annual trip. It would be another year before he had to go flying all over the world. He decided that it was time to take a short vacation. During his annual trip, he saw many beautiful places throughout the world but never had the time to stop and enjoy them. He decided to use his vacation time to see some of those sights. He had his chief elf book him a cabin on one of the cruise ships and he set off to enjoy himself.

When he arrived at the port there were dozens of ships in the harbor and he had some difficulty finding his. However, he was soon aboard and had his belongings stowed away. Then he went up on deck to watch as the large ships left the harbor for the open sea. He listened to the ringing bells as various passengers signaled for their porter and the captain signaled different commands. It was all quite fascinating to him.

Their first destination was an island in Australia. St. Nicholas watched in awe as the ships passed each other in the night and danced precariously with the Great Coral Reef.

The lighthouses on shore gave ominous warning to beware of coming too close. Santa went up to the bridge where the captain welcomed him. "We normally don't allow passengers on the bridge," the captain stated. "Since I know who you are, however, I'm willing to make an exception. After all, you know more about navigating than I do."

The captain ordered a course correction and the pilot made it amid sounding bells that notified the crew that they were changing direction. The course correction was necessary because they were very close to running aground on the reef. The large ship would have been nearly impossible to navigate in these waters without the assistance provided by the lighthouses. The lighthouses told the captain when he was nearing dangerous reefs and he was able to steer around them. St. Nicholas found the whole operation very fascinating. There were times when these same lighthouses had served as a beacon to him as well, except in his case they allowed him to know where he was at. His sleigh of course was much more maneuverable than the large ships that the lighthouses assisted but when one was flying in the dead of night any beacon was appreciated.

At last they arrived at their port of call. St. Nicholas listened as the bells sounded their approach and their departure from the ship. He had looked forward to this for a long time. "Thank you, Captain," St. Nicholas stated as he walked toward the gangplank. "I've been needing a vacation for quite a while now."

"We'll see you tomorrow night when the clock reaches seven St. Nicholas," the captain answered. "We'll leave harbor when we sound the bells."

The Year Mrs. Claus Delivered Christmas

Santa had a cold. It was no ordinary cold either. It was a magic cold. Anybody knows that a magic cold is the worst kind of cold. Therefore, Santa had a serious problem. It was one day before Christmas Eve and Santa was too ill to make his annual round the world trip! What was he to do? He had considered many options and all of them had fallen through. He had contacted his friend the Easter Bunny and found that the Easter Bunny too was ill. He had gone through his list of elves and none of them was qualified to take over for him. He had even gone so far as to contact the Grinch Who Stole Christmas and found that the Grinch was also ill.

"Mama," cried Santa to Mrs. Claus, "what am I to do? I have less than a day to find a replacement. If I do not, I will be forced to cancel Christmas. Just think of all the disappointed children we'll have if I fail them!"

"I'm sure something will work out," Mrs. Claus answered. "I'd deliver Christmas for you if I weren't so busy."

"That's it," Santa exclaimed. "You can deliver Christmas this year! I will go along in case you run into trouble. I will stay in the sleigh so I will not contaminate everybody on Earth."

"Now Santa," Mrs. Claus replied, "you know I cannot do that! I have to be here at home to supervise the elves while you're gone."

"Barney, the chief elf can do that," Santa replied. "He's more than qualified to keep an eye on things here. He's practically running the shop already."

"But who will prepare your meal for your return," Mrs. Claus asked. "Who will prepare your hot chocolate and make your bed?"

"June can do that," Santa responded. "She's actually the one who does those things anyway. You only supervise. If it makes you feel better, you can write out a set of instructions for her. She really will not need them though. She is very good at her job. You know that as well as I do."

"She should be good at it," Mrs. Claus replied. "I trained her to do it and she's done so for over two thousand years."

"So there you go," Santa answered. "I'll have no more arguing about it. You are going to deliver Christmas this year. If you do not, I'll be forced to cancel it."

"Okay Santa," Mrs. Claus replied. "I'll have to dig my suit out of the mothballs and have it altered to fit me. There isn't much time, so I best see to it right away."

"Howard," Santa called to his assistant. "Dig Mrs. Claus' suit out and have it altered to fit her. Also tell the elves to leave room in the sleigh for two passengers this year. Mrs. Claus is going to deliver Christmas. If I go into anybody's house, I will spread this magic cold to every human on the planet. It is bad enough that I have it. If it breaks out in the human population, I would be responsible for the deaths of millions of people. I am not willing to expose one single person to it. The last thing the world needs is a pandemic."

"But Santa," Howard asked, "won't Mrs. Claus spread it after being around you?"

"No," Santa replied. "As long as she is not ill herself, she won't. Magic colds only spread when the carrier has a fever. We will keep a close watch on her, but she should be okay. If she is not showing any symptoms, we will be okay. I am going to have Edward, the chief medical elf, examine her to be sure. I will also have him mix up some of his magic cold formula and then have her take it. If she is starting to come down with it, the formula will keep her from spreading the disease while she's exposed to humans."

"Won't the formula prevent you from spreading it as well," Howard asked. "You know how Rudolph and the other reindeer complain if you have more than one passenger."

"I'm sure they'll understand," Santa replied. "I'll talk to them and explain the situation if it will ease your mind however."

"Thank you," Howard said. "I don't want to have to deal with all the grumbling!"

Santa went to the stables where the reindeer were practicing their flying. "Rudolph," he called. "Can you come here? I need to have a word. Have all the team gather around as well."

"Dancer, Comet, Cupid, Blitzen, Prancer, and Malcomb," Rudolph called. "Can you all gather around. Santa needs to have a word with us."

"Malcomb?" Santa asked. "Why do you want Malcomb?"

"Because Dasher is ill," Rudolph replied. "He picked up a stone in his hoof. He will be too sore to go this year. We've trained Malcomb to take his place."

"I see," Santa responded. "Well, something like that is why I asked you all to gather here. I am not going to be able to deliver Christmas this year. I have a terrible magic cold. I either must cancel Christmas or else Mrs. Claus will have to go along. I know you all do not like pulling the sleigh with an added passenger, but it is my only option. I will not force you to do it though. It's strictly voluntary."

"We understand," Rudolph stated. "I believe I speak for each of the reindeer when I say we'll volunteer to do it. We know how important it is. We do not want you to cancel Christmas just because of a magic cold. On the other hand, we do not want to be responsible for releasing a pandemic on the human population. We care for the humans just as much as you do. Isn't that right guys?"

The remaining reindeer all shouted their agreement. Then Santa put out his hand and each of the reindeer laid a hoof on top of it. "On three," Rudolph called out. "One, two, three, Merry Christmas!"

Santa walked back to his office. He was met there by Howard. "The alterations have been completed on Mrs. Claus' suit," Howard told him. "It only needed a slight adjustment. Mrs. Claus has not gained but a few pounds in the hundreds of years since she wore it last. She really looks sharp in it. Have a look-see for yourself."

"Here I am," Mrs. Claus said from behind him. Santa turned in the direction of her voice. Mrs. Claus looked absolutely stunning in her suit. Santa could easily see why he had chosen to marry her. She was very beautiful, even at 2500 years of age. Her eyes were like two beautiful, green stars. Her raven hair hung most of the way down her back. Her button nose and bright smile topped off a beautiful, tapered chin. She looked the same as she had when he first met her nearly 3,000 years earlier.

"You look beautiful," Santa stated. "You're every bit as beautiful as you were the day, I met you. Do you remember that day?"

"Yes, of course I do," Mrs. Claus replied. "You were visiting my father, Father Time. He introduced us and I knew you were my future husband. I was right too, because you proposed on the spot. I thought you were being a bit presumptuous in proposing marriage to a woman you had just met. However, before I could think, I heard myself say yes. My father performed our ceremony on the spot. He told me later that he had known all along that you and I were destined to be together. Of course, that's no big deal for him because he knows the future since the future is part of him."

"How is your father?" Santa asked. "I haven't heard from him for nearly three months."

"Oh he's fine," Mrs. Claus answered. "He called the other day in fact. He is seeing Mother Nature again. I think they are going to reconcile. Father was torn up badly after the divorce. He never quit loving her. Mother knew it too. I think that is why she called on him and asked him to come see her. They've been seeing each other regularly ever since."

"Well, I for one would love to see them get back together," Howard replied. "They're meant for each other. Now I must go see to the last-minute arrangements before you all leave tomorrow night. I need to make sure the sleigh has provisions for two. I must also make sure you have the proper protection from the elements. It is extremely cold in some parts of the world. There is also a tropical gale blowing over the south Pacific. You will have to detour around it. Therefore, I have got to decide for the reindeer to deviate from the flight plan. If all goes well, you may actually cut a few hours off your travel time."

"I know we'll cut some time this year," Santa replied. "The reindeer have been working on a way to fly twice as fast. Besides that, Father Time has granted us the ability to distort time even more this year. He is providing us with some stable wormholes over North America and Europe. Those alone will allow us to shave six hours off our time. Mother Nature is also going to help. She is going to provide tail winds wherever we go. The tailwinds will propel us even faster. Last year the weather over

South America was very uncooperative. So, Mother Nature reprimanded the weather there and assures me that there will be good weather everywhere. She is also going to provide everybody with a white Christmas. Well, everybody north of Tennessee anyway. The other areas are much too warm for snow. She said she would see what she could do about providing snow even in the hot areas though."

"Santa," June the elf called. "I heard that Mrs. Claus is going with you this year. I want to assure you that everything will be prepared exactly as you like it when you return. I will also double the preparations to accommodate Mrs. Claus. I wanted to ask you if I could use Martha the elf as my assistant this year since the work will be doubled?"

"Yes you can," Santa replied. "Howard, have Barney reassign Martha to assist June. Tell him I approved the transfer. Now I must take Mrs. Claus to see Edward. I want to make sure she isn't going to spread this stupid cold."

A few minutes later, Edward was examining Mrs. Claus. "I'm certain she's been exposed," Edward told Santa. "Since she is a magical creature, there is no doubt that she'll come down with it. However, I will give her some medication to suppress it. The medication will keep it at bay for about a week. That will prevent her from spreading it to any humans. Now I suggest the two of you get some sleep. You have a big day tomorrow."

Santa left Edward's office and went to his quarters. Sleep came quickly since he knew that all was going to work out well.

The next day he awoke with a start. It was Christmas Eve, and they would be leaving on their run shortly. The whole run typically took twenty-four hours to complete. They would go across the Arctic Circle first, stopping in Greenland. Greenland did not have a large population but there were several Eskimo families living there along with some military families. They would visit each of them before going to Asia, then Europe, Africa, Australia, and then the Americas. It was not unusual for Santa to leave the North Pole at 6:00AM and return at 7:00AM on Christmas morning. "We'd better eat our breakfast and then prepare to leave," Santa told Mrs. Claus. "I appreciate you doing this for the children."

"The children are our very reason for existence," Mrs. Claus replied. "Of course, I'm willing to help."

They ate a hearty breakfast and then went to the docking bay to begin their trip. Santa climbed into the sleigh on the left side and watched as his wife sat down to his right. Then he picked up the reigns. "On Comet, on Cupid, on Donner, and Blitzen, on Dasher, on Dancer, on Rudolph, and Malcolm. Away!"

The reindeer took off down the launching tube at a gallop. In no time at all, the reindeer left the ground and the sleigh soon followed. Moments later they cleared the long launch tube and headed out over the frozen wasteland that made up the North Pole. In no time they were at their cruising altitude high in the clouds. Shortly thereafter, they landed next to an igloo in Greenland. True to her word, Mother Nature had provided a nice tail wind and they had made the trip from the North Pole to Greenland in moments. Mrs. Claus looked at Santa questioningly as they pulled up next to the igloo. "How am I supposed to enter an igloo if it has no chimney?"

"Just pick up the bag and a chimney will appear when you're in position," Santa answered.

Mrs. Claus picked up the bag and suddenly started floating to the top of the igloo. Just as Santa had said, a chimney suddenly appeared and swallowed her up. Before she could blink, she was standing in the center of the igloo. To her surprise, the igloo was quite warm. She reached into the bag and placed its contents under the makeshift tree, which adorned one corner of it. Then she instinctively lay her finger beside her nose and went up the chimney. Once she cleared the chimney, she was put down on the opposite side of the igloo!

"Santa!" Mrs. Claus called. "The bag put me down on the wrong side. Why did it do that?"

"Because you aren't finished yet," Santa answered. "Reach into the bag."

Mrs. Claus reached into the bag. She felt something huge. When she pulled it out, it was a kayak? She took the kayak out and placed it on the rack behind her. It was a replacement for the kayak that was already there. When she saw the old kayak, she remembered why she loved Santa so. The old kayak was tattered and in bad shape. It was far from being seaworthy. She took the old kayak down and placed it behind the kayak rack. Then the bag lifted her into the air, and she floated across the igloo and was placed in the sleigh next to Santa.

Thus, they continued their trip until well into the wee hours of the following morning. They returned to the North Pole two hours ahead of schedule. Mrs. Claus was ecstatic with the success of her first mission. An elf came to meet them and unhooked the reindeer from the sleigh. As the reindeer were led away, the sleigh began to be lowered to the second deck where it would remain until the following year. A team of elves waited for it there. They would go over it with a fine-tooth comb to make sure it was ready for the next trip.

"I have your cocoa waiting Santa," June stated. "Martha also has a cup of cocoa for you Mrs. Claus. "It's just the way you both like it. We have also laid out your pajamas and turned down your bed. You must be exhausted after your trip?"

"Yes," Mrs. Claus replied. "We're very tired. Cocoa sounds very nice and then going straight to bed afterwards sounds even better. Who knows? I may want to deliver Christmas again sometime. Say in perhaps a thousand years?"

PSYCHIC ENCOUNTER / HORROR

Psychic Encounter

I always knew I was gifted if you can call it a gift. I can tell if a house has a "history". In other words, I feel people who are between worlds. I do not like to use those terms though. I prefer to think in terms of psychic energy that is left behind. You see I am a reader. I "read" this energy. I have seen people murdered who lived centuries before me. There is one which sticks with me, however. A house I lived in someplace in Ohio gave me the creepy crawlers from the day I moved in. I was petrified of the basement, though I was not sure why. Strange things began to happen. We were sick with no apparent reason. We heard noises and often did things we would not normally do. This went on for some months. Fall came and it got worse. My mom was literally whipped by an unseen force. She had welts to prove it!

One night, we pulled into the driveway. Suddenly I got an impression of a little boy. He had been murdered there. I could see the killer and knew who it was. I also saw the little boy in my mind's eye. He was five or six years old. He wore an off-white shirt with red and yellow pin stripes. He had on sky blue shorts with white stripes on the legs. I knew where he was buried as well. I knew his name was Joey.

The next day, my wife drove me to the cemetery. She entered from the back, so the markers faced away from us. All at once, I told her to stop, for we were at his grave. I walked to the front of it. The marker had a picture of a six-year-old blonde boy wearing an off-white shirt with red and yellow pin stripes. He had on a pair of baby blue or sky-blue shorts with a white stripe. His name was George with "Joey" in quotes. I was flabbergasted to say the least!

I drove to the county seat and confirmed his mode of death. Then I went to the police! I got an officer who knew my history of mental illness, so I figured all bets were off. However, he remembered the little boy's death and had considered it suspicious. So, when I told him what I knew, he asked me how he could nail the killer. I told him to test the water in the child's lungs for something not found in city water or pool water. At the time, such tests were not standard procedure. I knew the child had drowned in stagnant water. The killer had told the authorities the child drowned in a swimming pool.

The officer had the test ran. The killer was confronted with the evidence and confessed to killing the child for insurance. After that, we moved. The next residents reported that the house was always quiet. Apparently, the demons that killed the child left when the child left.

I truly believe in energies remaining behind. I ask myself all the time what would have happened if I had not followed my heart with Joey? He lives on still as part of me.

Visitors

It was close to dinner time on Christmas Eve. My wife and I had just sat down with the family to eat Christmas dinner. It had been a tradition in our family to eat Christmas dinner the night before Christmas since I could remember. So, we sat down to follow tradition. Just as I sat down however, the doorbell rang. I got up and went to answer the door. When I opened the door, there was a vagabond standing there. "Sir," he asked. "I'm hungry. Could you spare a few dollars so I can get a bite to eat?"

"No," I answered him, "you would probably just buy a bottle of liquor with it anyway. The mission is just across town. If you go there, they will feed you and give you a place to sleep."

The vagabond started to say something, presumably in protest. I wanted no part of it. Instead, I shut the door in his face and went back to my dinner. "Who was there?" my wife asked.

"Oh, it was just a wino," I answered. "He was begging for money. I turned him away. I should have called the police."

As I was speaking, the doorbell rang again. I got up to answer it. When I opened it there was a bag lady standing there. "Can you spare a lady a sandwich?" she asked. "After all, it's Christmas and I'm hungry."

"No! I can't," I answered. "You'd probably use anything I give you for drugs anyway. If I give you food, you would feed it to the birds. The mission is just across town. I donate money there all the time and I know they'll feed you."

She too started to protest but I closed the door in her face and walked away. I sat down at my table and my wife again asked who it was. "Some bag lady," I answered. "She wanted a sandwich, but I knew she'd waste it by feeding it to the birds and feral cats. Anyway, I turned her away. She is lucky I did not call the authorities to lock her in an asylum. She's obviously insane."

As I was speaking the doorbell rang again. "Can't a family even eat in peace?" I asked as I went to the door. I was angry as I jerked the door open. My anger immediately gave way though when I saw an angel standing there, complete with the halo surrounding his head. "Come inside," I said. "Warm yourself by the fire. Pull up a chair at the table. We were just having our Christmas dinner. We'd love for you to join us!"

The angel pulled up a chair at the table and we did our best to make him feel welcomed. How often is it that one is visited by the messengers of God anyway? "So," the angel spoke. "It looks like you've done well in your lifetime. The lord has blessed you very much."

"Yes He has," I said. "I can't thank Him enough."

"What do you mean you can't thank Him enough," the angel asked. "You've already had two chances to have dinner with Him personally tonight and you turned Him away both times!"

Fiending

The young man was desperate. He had heard that the old woman had drugs in this place, and he needed some badly. He was trashing her house as she sat bound to a chair. He had considered gagging her but knew doing so would defeat his purpose. The old woman kept giving him clues. "You're cold," she would say, letting him know he was not even close.

He almost felt like an animal being trained. If he got close, she would reward him and if he were way off base, she would warn him. She was shaping his behavior. "Enough of the games old woman," he said. "I know you have drugs here and I want some. If you do not give them to me, I will steal your whole stash when I find them."

"You are getting warmer," she taunted as he moved from one side of the room toward the other. He figured that she was hinting that her stash was in the other room since he was close to the door.

"Go figure," he said to himself, "the old broad is pushing eighty and she's a drug dealer!"

"You're a little warmer now," the old woman said. "But you still aren't going to find my stash. I will make you a deal though. If you turn me loose and let me have my way with you, I will not only give you what you want, but I will keep you from being a total loser in the end. If you choose to continue this path however, I warn you there will be dire consequences!"

Now he was really mad! Not only was this old broad withholding the drugs he needed but she was also trying to have sex with him! Why, she was old enough to be his grandmother's grandmother! How dare she believe he would want anything to do with her. Why, the very thought disgusted him.

"What do you say Jimmy?" she asked. "Want to show an old woman a good time? You know, there may be snow on the mountain but there's still fire in the furnace!"

How did the old lady know his name? Jimmy knew he had never told her his name and he was certain she had never seen him before. Perhaps she knew him from the neighborhood. After all, they lived in the same part of town. Yes, that had to be it! Jimmy searched all through the kitchen cabinets. "You're nowhere near what you have coming," the old lady said.

"Well then, why don't you help me you old witch," he replied, "and tell me where you hid it."

"Oh no," she responded. "It's against the rules for me to help you find it. Those who get what I have in store for them must earn it and go to it willingly!"

Jimmy was really getting upset now. He was very dope sick and needed to find where she hid her stash. He began searching her bedroom. "You're getting warmer," she said. "In fact, you are getting hot!"

"Finally," Jimmy thought. "If I'm getting hot, the dope must be in this room."

He noticed a door to his left and decided to check it out. “You’re getting hotter,” the old lady said as he began to open the door.

He opened the door and found that it led to a tunnel through the house. “It would be like a drug dealer to have a hidden room in their house,” he thought.

He stepped inside and began walking through the tunnel. The door behind him abruptly closed. He followed the tunnel for some distance and looked back. Strange, he had walked a good way and yet the door was right behind him. He realized then that the walls were closing in on him. He tried to resist but it was futile. The floor opened beneath him and he found himself looking straight into hell. The walls pushed and he began plunging into the fire. “Now you’re really getting hot,” he heard the old woman say.

Jenkins Farm

I had been looking for work since the factory shut down. It had been months and I was beginning to wonder if I was ever going to find employment. I could just see myself sitting on a street corner with a white cane in my hand and a hat in front of me to feed my family. Not being quite that desperate however, I continued to look for work. My unemployment had long since run out and I did not qualify for any type of assistance. My next step would have to be to start dipping into my retirement or going to the poor house to borrow from my rich uncle.

One day, I had an idea. I took the necessary funds and bought a business license. Then I placed an ad online for odd jobs and waited to see if I got any responses. I had said in the ad that I was willing to do anything from yard work to mechanical work and anything in between. One day the phone rang. "Is this Calvin's Odd Job's?"

"Yes, it is," I replied.

"Would you be willing to do farm work? The work is hard, and the pay is low. However, it would be steady."

"Yes," I replied. "I'd be happy to do anything that is steady work."

"Well, show up at 4:00 AM tomorrow at the first house on Harmon Road. I own the farm there. It is a 300-acre spread, and I need to plow, till, and plant 150 of those acres soon. Have you ever run a farm tractor? If not, I will show you how. It is not hard really. You will not be any place where you can do much damage, so you will be fine. By the way, my name is Fred Harmon."

"I will be there at 4:00 AM Mr. Harmon," I answered.

"Call me Fred," He responded. "Mr. Harmon and sir were my father's names."

"Okay Fred."

The next morning, I drove to Fred Harmon's house on Harmon Road. It was easy to see why it was called Harmon Road. There were at least seven houses up and down the road, all owned by various members of the Harmon family. Fred's house was the last house on the left the way I went in. Had I approached from the other direction it would have been the first house on the right. However, I'd have had to have gone ten miles out of my way to go that way.

"You're right on time. I like that," a voice said from the side of the house.

I turned to see a muscular looking man with weathered features approaching. "I'm Fred Harmon. You must be Calvin Reed? Come with me and we will get right to work on those fields. With the whole crew plowing we should be able to have them plowed in one day."

"I do not know much about farming Fred, but I sure do not see how 2 men can plow 150 acres in one day!"

"Two men cannot. However, when you add in all my brothers and the men working for them, the two men becomes 25 or more."

It was then that I heard the sound of the first approaching tractor. "We help each other plow, till, and plant. Then if somebody needs help during harvest time, we send any men we can spare to help there too. You will get to know my brothers and sisters and their farms as well as I do."

"I noticed another farmhouse a few miles from here. Who owns that?" I asked.

"Oh, that is the old Jenkins place? I heard it was bought by a band of gypsies after old man Jenkins died. I wanted to buy it myself because it connects to my property just beyond the ridge line. Old man Jenkins had a dispute with my dad when I was just a kid though and never spoke to any of us again. He left it in his will that none of us were ever to buy his property. I heard there is a new family living there now. They bought it about five years ago. I hear some awfully strange sounds coming from over that way sometimes, but I don't know what they are."

Fred was right. By the end of the day, we had all 150 acres of his land plowed and over two-thirds of that tilled as well. It was little wonder though. There were nearly 40 tractors all lining up beside each other plowing and then tilling the land. It was an amazing feat of orchestration but when everybody did their part it worked out well. I found the big John Deere tractor intimidating when I first climbed into the cab, but Fred told me what to do and I was soon handling it like I had been doing so all my life. I figured the pay might not be the greatest, but I did not mind doing that until the factory reopened, if it did.

By the end of my first month, we had plowed, tilled, and planted every acre of every farm in the Harmon family. I was finding that I was actually very good at farm life. I had a few blisters but nothing major. My hands were calloused already. The few months of inactivity had softened them up a little, but

I had stayed active enough to keep most of my callouses. Now I was very glad.

One evening I was working over. One of the tractors had broken down and we had to get it repaired before morning. While I was working, I heard a sound in the distance. I could not make out what it was, but it sounded like a cross between a blood-curdling scream and a guttural growl. I dismissed it and went about my business. We finished the job and I started to drive home. As I approached the old Jenkins place, I saw a little girl standing on the side of the road. She flagged me down and asked for help. She said her mommy had been hurt. So, I pulled into the drive and parked my car. I walked into the house. Suddenly, I felt something stab me in the buttock. I turned to see a woman with a needle standing there before I lost consciousness. When I came to, I was buried up to my neck in the ground. I was gagged with duct tape. Two little girls were standing looking down at me. They held a skull in their hands. "Let's bake this one on the rotisserie Mommy," said one of the twins while pointing at me.

Hell, to Pay

Cynthia looked around at her lair. The look in her eyes was enough to wilt weeds. She hated it here but was bound. She could not leave even if she wanted to. It was just a small cubicle but at least it was her cubicle. She was familiar with it. In many cases that meant more than anything. There was nothing human about staying with the uncomfortable and the unhealthy long after one should have moved on. It was the trait of any being to resist change. Cynthia had resisted change for so long she could not remember the difference.

"What troubles you daughter?" Satan asked.

Satan was not the horned creature many believed him to be. In fact, he was quite handsome and perhaps even bordered on beautiful. He had to be. It was part of his lure. Therefore, Cynthia was equally beautiful. Her long black hair and big brown eyes had melted many hearts.

"Father, it's so dull around here," Cynthia replied. "Isn't there something I can do to liven things up a little bit?"

"It's not meant to be a pleasant place," her father answered. "It took a long time to make it as cruel as it is. However, if you wish to be entertained, I suggest finding some trouble to get into."

"That's just it," Cynthia replied. "I've already created as much mischief as I can think of. Yet I am so bored. These humans bore me."

"Then figure out creative ways to lead to their demise," her father answered. "I love watching them suffer the consequences of their foolishness. Surely you can find a human whose every wish you can grant in exchange for their soul?"

"I'll do it Father," Cynthia replied. "I'll find some sucker out there and give them whatever they want in exchange for their soul."

"That's my girl," Lucifer answered. "Go now and make your father proud! If you want, you can pay a visit to Frank Goins, 33214 South 216th Street. He has stated that he is willing to sell his soul to me for a chance to go back in time. Apparently, he has got the notion that if he were able to go back in time, he could look up his former self. Then, with his precise knowledge of the stock market and what stock did best on what day, he could become a millionaire many times multiplied. You are to provide him with safe passage to his youth. Cynthia, you know what to do. Have fun with him!"

"I will father," Cynthia said as she vanished into thin air in search of her target.

She found him asleep on his bed. He was an old man with an old man's pot belly and bald head. His eyes were mere beads sunk into his head. He looked a bit frightening to most people. Cynthia liked the look.

"Hello Frank," she said, waking him from his sleep. "Don't be afraid. I am not here to harm you. I just wanted you to know that your request has been heard. My father Lucifer wants to provide you the means to travel through time to your youth. We will transport you back to an era before the stock market crash of 1929 in exchange for your soul."

"I'm doomed anyway," Frank said. "I have nothing to lose. What do I have to do?"

"You simply sign this contract," Cynthia replied. "Then you'll go down to the bus station and give the driver the ticket I provide you with. From there, your wish will be granted. The bus will drive all night non-stop. When it arrives at your destination, it will be April 1929. You can do whatever you wish from there."

"What's the catch?" Frank asked. "We all know your father. He's always got an angle."

"There is no catch," Cynthia replied. "We'll transport you to 1929 and you do your thing from there. Once you die, you go directly to hell."

Frank did not hesitate to sign the contract, much to Cynthia's delight. She almost felt sorry for the man, but he would get what he deserved. Once the contract was signed, she gave him the ticket. Then with a wave of her hand the room disappeared, and they stood at the bus stop. She made sure he was aboard the bus and then grinned as she walked away. Her father would be so proud of her!

Frank found a seat at the back of the bus, and the bus was soon underway. Frank wanted to sleep but was much too anxious to do so. He went over his plans in his head. At some point along the way he became tired and drifted off to sleep. He slept for hours. When he awoke, he was no longer aboard a sleek new 21st Century bus. Instead, everything about him had changed and he was now aboard a much older bus. It appeared to be a bus from the early 1950's or possibly even prior to that. Something did not feel right, however. Frank could not quite place what it was, but something was wrong.

By morning, his transport had ceased to be a bus and he found himself in a turn of the 20th Century car. He asked the driver what the date was. He was informed that it was April 1, 1929. He looked down at his wrinkled hands and realized what had gone wrong. He had indeed been duped! The idea was so outrageous to him that he became very agitated. The excitement and shock were too much for him. Due to his age and his weakened condition, it caused him to have a heart attack. As he was dying, Cynthia appeared beside him. "What have you done?" he asked her.

"We granted your wish," she replied. "We transported you to 1929. We never once promised you that we'd arrange for you to live long enough to see your former self."

As she said this, Frank screamed in pain as flames began to engulf him. "Welcome to hell," Cynthia said with raucous laughter. Her father would be proud!

Frosty, the Ax Murderer

It was still early in the winter when the big blizzard struck. It snowed nearly three feet, which was perfect for building a snowman of course. Several of the town's kids got together and did just that. They built a huge snowman with two chunks of coal for eyes, a carrot nose, and several pieces of coal for a mouth. The one problem they had was that they could find nothing to use for arms. They had one nice stick but a snowman with only one arm. They looked around and came up with a solution. One of the little boy's father was a wood chopper. As such, he had several axes. They borrowed two of the axes and used them as snowman arms. A little girl suggested that they dress their creation. The snowman looked naked with only a corn cob pipe adorning him. When they all agree to dress him, one of the children suggested asking the old woman who lived in a nearby house for something to put on the snowman. It was said by some that she was a witch, but most people did not believe it. Most of the kids believed it though and they all refused to go except one brave little girl named Sally.

"Hello," the old lady answered as Sally stood at her door. "I see you children have built a nice snowman. I will bet you would like something to put on him, wouldn't you? Well, you came to the right place. The only thing I have, however, is an old hat. Put it on him and magic will happen."

She gave Sally the hat and Sally ran with it the group of waiting children. "That was awfully brave of you," said Benjamin. "So, what did the old witch say?"

"She gave me a hat to put on him," Sally answered. "She said the hat was magic."

"Well then she is a witch," Carolyn replied. "Maybe we should not use the hat?"

"It will be okay," James, an older child replied. "I don't believe in that hocus-pocus stuff anyway. She's probably just a mean old lady."

"Must not be too mean," answered Jenny. "She gave us a hat."

Sally pulled the hat out of the bag and they placed it on the snowman's head. Suddenly, the snowman's smile curled upwards into a scowl and the two lumps of coal became glowing red eyes. The snowman had come to life and he was not going to be nice! He wiggled a little and started to shake. "How dare you little hoodlums turn my beautiful snow into large balls," he asked. "You will all pay for doing so as will your families!"

With that said, he began to raise the axes above his head as the frightened and stunned children looked on. Once he had both axes above his head, he quickly buried the blade of the left ax into James' head, killing him instantly. "Now tell me you don't believe in hocus-pocus you little bastard," the snowman yelled. "They call me Frosty because not only am I made of snow, but my heart is ice cold!"

Most of the kids had now saw the seriousness of the situation and made good their escape. Along with James however, Frosty had managed to bury his axes in two more, killing one and fatally wounding the other. She was paralyzed as he had chopped into her back. It would take a few hours of excruciating pain until she died. Frosty realized this and the knowledge brought a credulous grin to his face.

"I'll kill every one of you kids," he bellowed after the now retreating children. "I'll kill everybody in this stinking town!"

He set out in pursuit of the children, sliding easily and with incredible speed across the snow. Moments later he beheaded a teenage girl and set out after a group of children who were outside the old woman's door, begging for their lives. The old woman opened the door but would not permit the children entrance. "I see you placed the magic hat on his head," the old woman said. "I told you that if you did, you'd find the results to be quite magical. I am going to use Frosty to make all your noisy little rug rats and your useless families magically disappear! Come and get the little brats my pet!"

Some of the children managed to escape but those who had run to the witch's house were all victims of her evil. The ones who escaped however made it to their homes and warned their parents. The parents did not want to believe them but the blood covering some of the children could not be denied. So, the parents sent for the constable, who arrived minutes later.

"Who did this?" the constable asked. "And don't feed me some story about a snowman coming alive."

"Why not?" a voice said behind him. "The story is true."

The next thing anybody knew the constable had blood squirting from his mouth as he crumpled to the ground. Before he died, he managed to turn and shoot a snowman.

The others quickly ran for the safety of the house. Frosty knew he would have to wait them out. If he went into the house, the heat would melt him. So, he waited. He waited for hours but they did not come out.

He decided that it was time to act, so he began to chop down the door. This led to his undoing though because a brave adult stood just inside the door by the wall. When the door gave way and Frosty entered the premises, the man grabbed the hat from Frost's head. Frosty immediately became just a simple snowman, melting on the man's floor.

Santa's Surprise

The little girl stood in line waiting for her turn to see Santa. She had watched the town Christmas parade with great anticipation of seeing the bearded elf afterwards. Now she had to endure the cold weather for her turn to sit on the old elf's lap and tell him her story. After waiting what seemed an eternity, her turn finally arrived.

"Come and sit on my lap darling," the old elf called to her.

She went to him and he picked her up, plopping her down on his lap.

"What is your name Sweetheart?" he asked.

"I thought you already knew my name," she responded. "Mommy tells me that you know the names of all the little boys and girls all over the world."

"Well I do," Santa answered. "I just like to have the child tell me as a conversation starter."

"Okay," the little girl replied. "My name is Audra. I live at 21547 East 45th Street."

"Yes," Santa replied. "I know your building well. I ripped the seat of my trousers there last year when I got off my sleigh. They got caught on an exhaust pipe sticking through the roof. You should ask your landlord to put a vent cap on it before somebody really gets hurt or a pigeon decides to make a nest in it. If a pigeon uses it for a nest, somebody may be harmed by exhaust fumes."

"I'll have my mother speak to the landlord about it," Audra answered. "After all, we would not want you getting hurt when you sneak in at night would we?"

"What can Santa bring you this year Audra?" the jolly old elf asked the young girl.

"Oh, I don't think you'll be bringing me anything this year," Audra replied knowingly. "However, there is something I want."

"Just name it," said Santa. "I'll do my very best to see to it that you get it."

Peltandra answered, "I want my mommy to quit cheating on my daddy. You see, she thought I was asleep last night when she had her boyfriend over. I watched as she kissed him and did a whole lot of other things that adults do."

"Oh you shouldn't watch things like that," Santa replied. "What adults do is not for children to see. It's private and should never be watched by children."

"Well I saw it," Audra replied. "I saw everything. I know exactly who the man was too. I have not told my daddy. I decided I would take care of things myself. I'm going to see to it that my mommy never cheats with the man again."

"I see," replied Santa. "You want me to prevent your mommy from cheating with this man then, is that it?"

"No," replied Audra. "I'll see to it that he never touches my mommy again. I just want you to know that I know who he is and that is why I'm doing what I'm going to do."

"Who is he?" asked Santa, wondering if there was something he could say to help the little girl.

"You already know the answer to that question as well," Audra answered. "You see, I know it was you kissing my mommy. I fully intend to stop you."

"How do you know it was me?" Santa asked.

"I recognized your voice," Audra answered. "I also heard you telling Mommy that you were Santa in the parade today."

"Well Honey, your mommy and I have a special relationship," Santa answered. "We're both adults and though you may not approve, we don't need your permission."

"I know that," Audra required. "That's why I'm going to take drastic action to save my mommy and daddy's marriage."

With that said, the little girl reached into her coat, pulled out a knife, and quickly slit Santa's throat.

FANTASY AND SCIENCE FICTION

Arrival

I had just recently been reassigned as part of my military duty. My new assignment was not of this world. I was assigned to a colony on Mars. Alpha One Port was a science colony on Mars. Its mission was to gather information about the red planet and send it back to scientists on Earth. Man planned to colonize Mars one day but doing so was impossible at that time. Mars was subject to storms with winds that made the category five hurricanes of earth look like nothing more than dust ups. The atmosphere on Mars was also poisonous and the climate uninhabitable. The mission of the scientists assigned there was to find solutions for all these problems. Companies on Earth were paying out large amounts of money to solve the many problems with colonizing Mars. I was assigned as part of a squad of grunts meant to police the scientists and solve any issues that might arise. It was a dull job. The most excitement we usually got was to listen to scientists banter with each other about things that were far beyond us.

It was the year 2245. Christmas season had just started on Earth. I knew that this was going to be another of those years when I would spend Christmas in a state of deployment. My family would miss me, and I would miss them. The scientists on Mars did not celebrate Christmas. Most of them considered themselves too intelligent for religion, others simply did not want to take the time off. So, Christmas was going to be just like any other day for me. It would be boring. There was a freighter coming in from Earth that day. To escape some of the boredom, I volunteered to help off load it and put the goods in storage. I watched as the freighter blasted its way to a landing.

"Airlock is secured," the computer announced in its mechanical voice as the ship docked. "Proceed with unloading of passengers."

The squad and I entered the airlock and tapped the controls to open the airlock of the freighter. The airlock opened and the inside of the freighter appeared to be pitch dark before us. Thinking it unusual to be met with such conditions, I held up my hand to stop the men from moving forward. Then I rolled my fingers into a fist, which was the silent signal to my men that I considered the situation unusual and a possible threat. I did not have to look to know that each of the men set his weapon for "stun" at that point. If we encountered any hostiles on board the freighter, we would attempt to subdue them before setting our weapons to the "kill" setting. I then signaled the men to advance and PFC Florence, a red headed marine from Texas took point. He entered the freighter and found the control panel for the lights. Soon the interior of the cargo bay was flooded in red lighting as the lighting cut in.

I heard something beyond the cargo bay doors and signaled for four of the men to check it out. I watched cautiously as they pressed themselves against the wall on either side of the bulkhead. One of them toggled a switch and the cargo bay door withdrew itself into the wall leaving a large opening to exit the bay and see the interior of the ship. What awaited there was a surprise to even the most seasoned soldier. The floors of the passageway were covered in a blanket of snow. The entire ship was decorated with Christmas decorations. In fact, there were more Christmas decorations on board the ship than I had seen in most cities on Earth. Standing in a control room just across from the cargo bay was what appeared to be a man. This was not any ordinary man though. This man appeared to be some sort of cookie, perhaps a gingerbread man. He motioned for us to enter the ship and the squad I had sent proceeded to secure him. I ordered the rest of the platoon to back them up since the situation was way beyond suspicious. I left a soldier to secure the cargo hold. I approached the cookie man thinking that this was probably just a hoax. After all, it was Christmas season on Earth. It was likely that somebody on board the ship had programmed the computer to emit a holographic image of a gingerbread man and all the Christmas decorations on board. Holographic technology had advanced enough that holographs looked and even felt real. The only way to tell the difference was to scan them with a sensor.

"Sir," Private Barnes reported. "I think there's a problem with the sensor. It says that this gingerbread man is a living, sentient being."

"That's because he is a living, sentient being," a voice to the right of me said.

I turned to see a man dressed in a Santa Claus costume standing there. "How did you get in here?" I asked. "How did you slip past the pickets?"

"It's my job to get into places unnoticed," Santa Claus answered. "My name is Kris Kringle. Some people call me St. Nicholas or Santa Claus. I heard that this bunch of Martian scientists was trying to establish the Mars colonies without Christmas. I have come to bring the Christmas spirit to Mars. Now if you will be so kind as to help us, we have a ship full of supplies, gifts, and other things to off load. I would like to get my reindeer off first. They will need to go take care of business. Do not worry. The Martian atmosphere will not hurt them a bit. After all, they survive the time they spend in San Francisco every year just fine."

I looked at this man with disbelief. Then he put his finger beside his nose. A fireplace suddenly appeared in the bulkhead wall and he flew up it like a flash!

Weary Sun

Apollos the Sun god awoke to make his daily trip across the sky from east to west. He had noticed of late that his energy was dwindling. He was not sure what that meant. What he did know however was that he was tired of hauling his chariot out every day and driving it in a mad fury across the sky. His father Chronos had told him to do so from an early age and he had never questioned it. Now however he had been doing it day after day for months and there seemed to be no reward in sight. He decided he was going to start making his trips a little shorter each day. Maybe if the trips became short enough the other gods and the humans who lived on Earth would appreciate him more. Apollos knew that it was not in his nature to feel that way but for some reason he did. As far as he knew, nobody had poisoned him with ambrosia, but one could never be sure. He decided to have a talk with some of the other gods and see if any of them were feeling poorly as well.

"I've been feeling a little poorly myself," answered Adonis, god of agriculture.

"Of course you have," said Pluto, god of the underworld. "Each of you have been cursed and will die. There is nothing you can do about it. Once you are in the underworld, you will be my prisoners for eternity and I will be king of the gods!"

"We'll see about that," Apollos replied. "You seem to forget who you're dealing with. Even if we become your prisoners in the underworld, stripped of all our powers, we will still have all the knowledge and wisdom we have accumulated over countless eons. We will escape. You mark my word."

The gods all succumbed to the curse placed on them by Pluto. Apollos could only manage to keep his chariot in the sky for a few hours each day. The day was much shorter as a result and the earth became very cold. Adonis also retreated completely and finally succumbed to Pluto altogether. Apollos knew there was only one thing he could do to save himself and the other gods. He had to feed them. Gods of course live on the worship they receive from mankind. So, Apollos sent Hermes, the messenger god, to talk to all the leaders of mankind. A large feast was organized in honor of the gods and the people would worship for days. Apollos knew that Pluto would never quit trying. The best the gods could do against his evil was strike a balance. He would weaken them once per year and even kill some of them. The worship of man would revive them all. It would take Apollos some time to recover each time, but he would once again warm the earth. Adonis would once again bless the earth with new growth. Life would start over.

Time Traveler

Sam read these words as he sat in his command chair. "People sure feared it, didn't they mother?"

"Yes Captain," his wife answered. "They most certainly were. However, you must remember that the pandemic of 2020 was over 200 years ago. The technology to eradicate it did not exist then. People were dying from it. Death was not eradicated until half a century ago. People back then thought of death as something negative. How would they ever have imagined that not dying would cause so many problems?"

"I know exactly what you mean Lieutenant," he answered using his wife's rank instead of saying "Mother" as he normally did. "If this mission fails the world will be doomed to overwhelming inflation and hunger."

"Yes Mother," he answered while looking at his own emaciated frame in the view screen. "Set time parameters for April 10, 2020. Location: COVID-19 epicenter. Let us hope we can become infected. Engage."

WESTERNS

The Bereaved

Tod saddled his horse and rode off toward the massive Square W ranch to the east of his own ranch. His best friend Clarence Wilson owned the "Square", as it was known in those parts. Now Clare lay dying. He had asked the younger Tod to come over today. He had said it was important. So, Tod was doing as his friend had asked. Just a few days prior, he had accepted the responsibility of tending to Clare's children after the dying man passed. It was sad to see such a once vibrant and healthy man waste away into nothing. The tumor had developed quickly, and Clare had gone quickly as well. The older Clare was only 42. Even for an era when death often found people early, it was young.

Clare was leaving behind four children. The oldest child was eleven-year-old Clare Jr. The next son was nine-year-old Jonathan. He was followed by Clare's oldest daughter Elizabeth who was seven. Last of all was five-year-old Cindy. Tod loved the children very much. When Clare had asked him to look after them, Tod did not hesitate to accept. Tod and his wife Jane had no children of their own because Jane was barren. She too loved Clare's children and was willing to raise them. They had known the children for most of the children's lives. In fact, they had been present the night Clare's wife Ellie had died giving birth to Cindy.

Tod wrapped Thunder's reins around the hitching post and climbed the steps to the porch of the Square W ranch house. It was a good size house but simple in design. Clare had built most of it himself. He had had some help but did most of the construction on his own. This was usually the case on the frontier known as the American west.

Tod was surprised to find the local judge sitting in the parlor when he entered the house. He knew that Clare did not care much for politicians. In fact, Clare had been heard to say that this politician was nothing short of a liar and con man. Tod agreed with Clare's assessment of the judge. Hence, Tod was surprised to see him there. In fact, Clare had often referred to the judge as Old Windbag. Clare however, kept the judge on retainer because he was the only lawyer in town. If he was here, Clare had sent for him.

"How are you doing Tod?" the judge asked. "I wanted to tell you I really think what Jane and you did for the Wilson kids is fantastic. It is not too many couples who would be willing to take on all four of them like that. I was concerned about placing them because I figured I would have to split them up. Why just recently I completed an adoption..."

"I am sorry to cut you off your honor, but Clare asked me to come over about now. Is he awake?"

"Yes he is," the judge answered. "I'd hurry though. I do not think he will be with us much longer. The doc is with him now."

Tod didn't wait for Old Windbag to finish speaking. Instead, he went up the stairs to his friend's room. He knocked on the door then went in without awaiting a response. Clare was sitting up in bed which surprised him. He had expected to find him asleep or worse based on the judge's words.

"Hello Clare," Tod stated. "You asked me to come over today at this exact time. Was there some particular reason?"

"Yes," Clare replied. "I wanted you to get here after Old Windbag got here. I wanted to change my will. I left the Square to you Tod. Now before you go to rearing let me explain. I figured that since you adopted my young'uns, you would need the added income the Square can provide you. The land itself is worth several hundred thousand dollars. However, you can make your real money from the beef you raise. Just last year alone I cleared nearly one million dollars in livestock sales. If you want to turn it over to Junior when he is older, you're welcome to do so. However, there are land grabbers coming around these parts now and they would figure out a way to swindle him out of it. He is much too young and inexperienced to operate a spread like this. You'll do well with it."

"Clare, I won't argue with you about it," Tod replied. "You're too ornery a cuss and it wouldn't help anyway. So, I'll take it."

"Thank you," Clare replied. "Now you'd better send the young'uns in. I hear angels singing Tod. It's time for me to go meet my Maker."

Tod sent the children in as Clare had asked then started to leave. Clare stopped him. "Where are you going Tod? You are part of this family too! I want you to stay in here. Besides the young'uns will need you directly."

Clare then blessed each of his children. When he finished, he snuggled down into his bed, lay his head on his pillow, and breathed his last. Tod had been present at the deaths of others, so he knew even before he called the doctor back into the room that Clare was gone. "I'll call James Kendall," Tod told the doctor.

James Kendall was the town undertaker. Tod had dealt with him a few times in the past. Kendall wasn't a bad person, but Tod couldn't see himself befriending the man anytime soon because of his profession.

"Katy," Tod asked the operator. "Can you get me James Kendall? Clare Wilson just passed."

"Oh my," the operator answered. "Please express my condolences to the children. Yes! I'll put you right through!"

Tod made the final arrangements. There was not a whole lot to be done. Clare had pretty much seen to everything himself. He had prepaid the funeral, selected his own coffin, selected the hymns to be sang during the service, paid the preacher to preach his funeral, paid the grave diggers who would bury him, and selected the three-piece suit that he was to be buried in. The only thing Tod had to do was schedule the service. It was decided that the funeral would be in two days. The body was to be embalmed and then lie in state at the house for a wake which was to be held the following day.

Tod wanted so badly to grieve the death of his best friend, but he would not permit himself to do so in the presence of Clare's children. Clare had been much more than a friend to Tod. He had been like a father. In fact, Clare had been closer to him than his real father had been. It had been Clare that taught Tod about religion and converted him to Christianity. Clare had been the best man at his wedding to Jane. Clare had co-signed the note he had taken out to buy his own ranch, the Lazy T. In fact, Clare had even come up with the name of the Lazy T. The word "lazy" Clare had arrived at while watching an old cur dog laying on somebody's porch. The "T" was short for Tod. Thus the "Lazy T". So, Clare had been much more than a friend. Tod could not properly think of a word that would sum up what Clare had been to him. He knew he had to though because it had fallen to him to give a eulogy. It was a task he was honored to perform.

Tod was concerned for Clare's oldest son, Clarence Jr. While the rest of the children had broken down upon their father's passing, Junior had simply walked away indifferently. While psychology was still in its infancy as a field of science, Tod knew that Junior's behavior was abnormal. Tod had done his best to console the three younger children. Then he had gone to look for Junior. He found his new son in the kitchen preparing to eat a sandwich.

He wanted to shout, "Are you silly or something? Your father just died and all you can think to do is eat?"

Instead, he simply joined the lad in eating and tried to get the boy to talk. "Folks will be coming by with all kinds of food tomorrow," Tod stated. "Miss Katy said she'd be by first thing in the morning with a basket of her famous fried chicken. I am sure you can count on the Widow Daniels to bring those noodles you like so well. The Foster twins will likely bring their German chocolate cake. You know, I don't know about you, but I still can't tell them girls apart."

"That's easy," Junior replied. "Samantha has darker hair than Sabrina and Sabrina is heavier than Samantha."

"I'll bear that in mind," Tod replied. "Maybe I won't embarrass myself by calling one of them the other's name. And Junior, I want you to know that I cannot say I know what you are going through because I do not. I am not in your skin. However, I am here for you. I will always be here for you. I know I am not your Pa. I never could be. However, I am going to do my utmost to see to it that none of you children ever want for anything. Then when you get a little older, I am going to turn the Square over to you. You are the rightful heir. Your Pa just wanted me to mind things for you until you got a little older."

"I know," Junior replied. "Pa told me he was leaving it to you. I told him to go ahead. Ma always wanted that I should get an education. I figured I would go to school, then maybe go to some university somewhere. That would make Ma real proud."

"Sounds fine to me," Tod replied. "You've already completed fifth grade. Before long, you will be in high school. If you apply yourself and work hard, you should have no problem getting into a good university. Have you considered what university you'd like to attend?"

"Harvard," Junior answered, "or maybe Princeton."

"Those are mighty fine schools," Tod answered. "I'm sure they'd accept a promising young man like yourself. Have you considered what you'd like to study?"

"I've been reading about a doctor who has started a field of medicine treating people with mental illnesses," Junior said. "His name is Sigmund Freud. I think that is what I want to do as well. I can always hire somebody to look after the ranch for me if you give it to me. Well, I think I will turn in now. I have a long day tomorrow. Pa has been after me for a while to ride out to the north pasture and scout watering holes for the drive coming up. I am going to do that tomorrow."

"Junior," Tod said gently, "the watering holes on the north pasture will have to wait. Your Pa's wake is tomorrow, and the funeral will be the following day."

"How was it that Jesus put it?" Junior asked. "Let the dead bury their own dead?"

"I don't think He quite meant it that way," Tod replied. "I think that was a reference to sinners burying their dead. I think Jesus was saying that we should not let anything interfere with or come before serving Him. I also think Jesus would agree with a son attending his father's wake on a day when there is no church service."

"Well, I promised Pa that I would get those watering holes scouted. Now Pa told us that you had adopted us. I reckon that makes you my step-pa. As such, if you are ordering me to attend the wake, then I will attend it. Otherwise, I am scouting watering holes!"

"No Junior, I'm not ordering you to attend the wake," Tod replied. "However, I am asking you to."

He could see from the expression on the boy's face that he was wasting his breath. He was not concerned that the boy would miss part of the wake. He was concerned that the boy might be by himself half a day's ride away when reality came home to him. It was obvious that Junior was in denial about his father's death. Tod wanted to be there to help pick up the pieces when the walls came crumbling and the boy's heart shattered. Obviously, the only way he could do that was by riding the range with the lad. So, he told Junior he would ride with him. Then they both went to bed.

Tod awakened early the next morning and went to Junior's room to check on him. He found the boy's bed made and the boy himself missing. So, he hurried to the corral to get his horse and ride off in search of him. When he got to the corral, he found the boy saddling a horse.

"I didn't want to wake you," Junior said. "I figured you'd catch up to me."

"Are you sure I can't talk you out of this?" Tod asked.

Just then a wagon came up the narrow stretch of road. It was James Kendall bringing the body back for the wake. Tod then saw the look of recognition on Junior's face. The boy fell to his knees in a heap of tears. Tod was heartbroken to see the boy in such turmoil but relieved to know that healing could now begin. He went to the lad's side. Junior embraced him and held him tight as the tears flowed from his eyes. The boy was devastated.

He cried for a good twenty minutes. Tod never once let go. He simply let the young man grieve.

The wake went well for a wake. Tod was bothered somewhat by all the laughter he heard around him at times. Did people not realize that this was not a happy time? Then Tod remembered what Solomon had written thousands of years earlier about being glad in a house of mourning. He could no longer be angry with those attending the wake. After all, he knew without a doubt that Clare was now celebrating. Why should people not be rejoicing? Another saint had just finished his race and was now at home in heaven.

Gunner

Tom stooped in front of his horse. The tracks in the mud clearly led west toward Hole in the Wall. He knew that if he allowed his bounty to get in there, he would be unable to capture him. He wanted to capture him so he could see him hanged for his crime. The bounty was an outlaw named Sam Gunner. Gunner was an appropriate name for the outlaw because he gunned down any man who stood in his path. Tom had no intention of being the next man Gunner shot. He knew that Gunner would put up a fight and that was exactly what Tom wanted. Despite that, Tom planned on doing all that was in his power to keep from killing Gunner. There was no doubt in Tom's mind that he could outshoot the outlaw. Yes, the outlaw was fast. He was lightning fast. Those who had witnessed the shooting earlier that night said they did not see Gunner go for his Colt. It had happened in a flash. One second, Bill Wilson was standing there ready to draw on Gunner and the next Bill was dying on the floor as Gunner kicked the pistol away from Bill's grasp. So, Tom knew that Gunner was indeed fast. Tom also knew that he himself was the fastest gun in the territory. If Gunner were smart, which Tom knew he was not, Gunner would surrender, and Tom could take him back to town for a fair trial before stretching his neck. Tom also knew that Gunner was not known to be smart. Fast hands did not equal brains. After the shooting, a posse had formed expecting Tom to lead them. Tom was the marshal of the territory. Instead, Tom had sent the posse home. Gunner was too fast for most of the cowhands that had wanted to come. Tom was not willing to get any of them killed.

He heard a horse ahead and knew it was Gunner. He could not make him out yet, but he knew it was him. He was not more than fifty yards ahead. To Tom's delight Gunner had ridden into a box canyon with sheer cliffs on each side. There was no place for the gunman to hide and no way to escape. Tom also knew Gunner well enough to know that Gunner knew his way around as well as Tom did. If he had ridden into a box canyon, he had done so intentionally.

"Gunner, I know you're up there and you know I'm back here. Why don't you surrender and make this much easier? I do not want to shoot you. If I shoot you, then you will not be able to ride back to town for a trial."

"You sound like there is going to be a trial, Tom. Don't I need to be there for that to happen if it is my trial? Why don't you just ride up here and get me?"

Tom entered the mouth of the canyon cautiously. He could see Gunner's silhouette in the darkness some twenty yards ahead. To get a non-lethal shot, Tom needed to be closer. He dismounted his horse and low crawled until he was close enough to see Gunner clearly. Gunner was still out in the open. In the interest of justice, Tom wanted a fair fight.

"Stand up Tom," Gunner said. "You know as well as I do that, I want to shoot you standing."

Tom stood up with Gunner clearly in his line of sight by the light of the moon. Gunner made his play and Tom fired from his hip, faster than he had fired before. He hit Gunner in his gun hand and Gunner's weapon fell to the ground. Gunner tried to pick it up again but found he could not.

"You shot my hand? Why did you not kill me?"

"I didn't kill you because I want the hangman to do it," Tom answered. "In case nobody told you Bill Wilson, the man you killed, was my father."

"I had to kill him Tom. He drew on me."

"We'll let the judge and jury sort that out," Tom replied as he pulled the outlaw's hands in front of him and handcuffed them.

"Tom, I sure wish you had just killed me. There is nothing quite as humiliating as listening to the whole town singing, hootin', and hollerin' while somebody is about to get their neck put in a noose. Now that somebody's going to be me."

"Shut up and get on your horse before I gag you."

Gunner stepped into the saddle as Tom held the bridle. Just as Gunner was about to throw his leg across the horse, he stopped and suddenly kicked backwards. Tom was ready for this and used the butt of his pistol to knock Gunner out, draping his unconscious body across the horse and tying him securely. Gunner came to a few minutes later. "Untie me Tom. I promise I will not try anything else. This is worse than being hanged will be."

"Well I guess you'll be humiliated both ways then."

Tom took the lead to Gunner's horse and rode off to town.

When he got to town he rode directly down the street. The town jail was on the other end of the street. It was now daylight. The streets were crowded as people stood around talking about the happenings of the night before. When Tom approached with

Gunner draped across his own horse, somebody asked if they should fetch the undertaker. "No," Tom answered. "Fetch the doctor. Gunner here needs his hand tended to. He has a bullet wound to his gun hand."

"Do what?" Jim Houser, the saloon owner asked. "Are you saying you shot Gunner in the hand, draped him across his own horse, and brought him back? Ha, ha, ha, ha!"

"Thanks Tom," Gunner said. "Much obliged."

"Don't mention it. Pleasure was all mine."

ESSAYS

Substance Abuse Disorder

Substance Abuse Disorder is a condition with which I am very familiar. You see, I have sat on both sides of the couch when it comes to substance abuse. I suffered from my personal addiction that lasted nearly 30 years and I am a dependency disorder major holding an associate degree with high honors in the field.

My substance abuse started out quite innocently. The first substance I ever abused and became addicted to was tobacco. I began smoking when I was nine years old. My dad smoked and it was easy to steal cigarettes from him. The first time I ever smoked a cigarette was when an adult gave me a cigarette. I did not realize at the time that he was trying to win my confidence so he could molest me. I was fortunate because my parents intervened before he could do so and told the man he would have to leave. He was a fugitive from justice and was hiding out in an old building we had. When we discovered him there, he told my parents why he was there and convinced them to let him stay for a few weeks. My father had a soft spot for fugitives because my father had been imprisoned for a crime it was later proven he did not commit.

So, when this man showed up in a building up the road from our house my parents let him stay. He quickly befriended my brother and I, paying particular attention to me. I was only nine years old, so I knew nothing of sex yet and had only just began to enter puberty. He took advantage of my naivety and began to lead me down a path of delinquency. Cigarettes were part of that path for him. I remember very clearly the first time he handed me a cigarette and had me smoke it. I did not really want to smoke it, but he said that real men smoked. So, I took a puff off the cigarette he offered and inhaled deeply as he said. I know now that my immediate reaction was a dopamine rush of major proportions. I literally had an orgasm as well as urinating in my trousers at the same time because of that one hit of nicotine. It is for that reason that when I began studying addiction as a student after many years of suffering from it, that I bought into the genetic model of addiction. According to this model, addiction has a genetic component in which a gene is tripped in addicts that many people never deal with. There was a study done of individuals using Positron Emission Topography or PET scans. PET scans are images of the brain which show areas of the brain that are active versus areas that are not active. In this double-blind study, participants were given a dose of a controlled substance such as marijuana, cocaine, or other substances. Half of the participants were given a placebo. The participants were then subjected to PET scans to determine the effect the substances had on brain activity. The results showed that a portion of the participants had huge dopamine surges throughout the cerebral cortex while others receiving the same amount of the substances barely had activity at all. Since dopamine is the brain's natural feel-good chemical, it makes sense to assume that addicts are trying to recapture that dopamine rush. The problem is that this dopamine release is often a once in a lifetime experience. Even when it is recaptured, it lessens with each dose of the drug that originally caused it, requiring higher and higher amounts to be taken until finally no amount of the drug will bring the desired dopamine release. Some substances such as crack cocaine and methamphetamine cause such a large initial release of dopamine that users experience orgasms such as the one I experienced when I first inhaled nicotine. In retrospect, my reaction would have been expected since nicotine is the most powerful stimulant in the world, much more powerful even than cocaine or methamphetamine.

The dopamine theory of addiction is that addicts have a genetic abnormality leaving them susceptible to addictive substances. Once the substance is introduced, the addict has an immediate and very intense dopamine reaction running from the anterior cerebral cortex to the posterior cerebral cortex. This pleasurable experience is so intense that many literally do experience it as an orgasm. The addict then tries to reproduce the feeling by reintroducing the same substance. They can capture some of the effect, but the original effect is never captured again. Many addicts have referred to this as "chasing the buzz".

In some cases, the addict is able to reproduce some of the initial effects, but the feeling is fleeting. Recapturing it takes higher and higher amounts of their drug of choice. This elusive effect leads to the addict using more and more of the drug. Thus, tolerance seems to be a condition found only in addicts. Many addicts, including I have made the statement that our bodies were designed to process chemicals. We seem to have an innate ability to tolerate with impunity dosages of drugs that would devastate or even kill people of the same weight and age. My drug of choice for example was the antihistamine Benadryl. Many would argue that Benadryl is not addictive and depending on how one defines addiction, it may not be. If one limits addiction to individuals who show classic withdrawal symptoms such as cravings, muscle cramps, nausea, irritability, etc. then Benadryl is not addictive. If you broaden the definition though and allow for the fact that withholding huge amounts of Benadryl after prolonged use of the drug results in a major histamine reaction due to the body's dependence on the drug as opposed to its own resources, you have another type of withdrawal.

I also exhibited classic tolerance to the drug when I was taking it. For most people, Benadryl simply results in sleepiness. Therefore diphenhydramine, the active ingredient in Benadryl, is so often used in OTC sleep products. For most people, 50mg of the drug is enough to induce sleep and they simply sleep it off. I took as much as 5000mg of the product at one time and simply got high on it. Admittedly, there were often when I found I had trouble walking because of taking such high dosages, so I usually found a place where I could sit comfortably for several hours as the effects subsided. Many medical professionals still do not believe that it is possible to take the amounts of the product I took and survive. However, research is becoming available in which others have reported taking extremely high amounts of the product and surviving. Benadryl is often the recreational drug used by inmates because many institutions have it on their list of acceptable products. In fact, many jails and prisons will sell it to inmates. Now that the secret is out about it though, fewer and fewer institutions are allowing the product to be purchased.

Addiction for me was much more than simple dependency on a chemical though. It entailed a mindset and a lifestyle. As a person, I was completely self-centered and anti-social. In fact, my early mental health diagnosis was anti-social personality disorder. It revealed itself in all my actions. As many addicts have been known to say, "If I wasn't getting dope from you or having sex with you then I wasn't dealing with you." I hated all authority figures passionately. Much of my life was spent in isolation and when I was in public, I was often too high to effectively interact with people. I left destruction everywhere I went, usually in the form of broken hearts and ruined lives. There are still people to this very day who will not speak to me because of the things I did to them. My actions were almost always unethical, if not illegal. The laws I did not break were badly bent. My ex-wife still does not fully trust me to this very day even though I have been in recovery for over eight years.

My recovery journey was using a twelve-step program. I do not mean to advocate any belief that twelve step programs are the only road to recovery. They were simply my road to recovery. Due to the traditions of the programs, I choose not to say which programs I was involved in. The programs helped me sort out the emotional wreck I had become, reclaim my life, and accept responsibility for my past. I do not regret having been an addict. It has given me a unique perspective on life and made me what I am today. I do not recommend it as a path for anybody because many people never recover. Denial is one of the classic symptoms of addiction. Those who accept the disease model of addiction often say that it is a disease which tells you that you do not have a disease. I cannot count the number of times I have said I could quit anytime I wanted to, I just did not want to. Those words came back to bite me. Addiction is a serious disease, and until it becomes a problem for the addict, it is not a problem.

Childhood Trauma

I was not one of those fortunate people who grew up in a perfect home as a child. My childhood started out very rocky and continued to get worse as I grew older. While I will not say I wish these events had not occurred, I can see how they have influenced my life. I can clearly see how they have had both a positive and negative impact on my life.

Though my family all lives in a state of either outright denial of the situation or at best wishes to sweep it under the rug and pretend it did not happen, what I am about to relate is true.

I lost my younger sister when I was around 12 years of age. She died from Sudden Infant Death Syndrome, which science now knows is due to using a used crib mattress. Her death naturally and deeply affected my father who was never good at dealing with death anyway. As a result, he began drinking heavily and plummeted into chronic alcoholism. As such, he became very abusive. Since he and I had never really had a great relationship to begin with, matters between he and I grew much worse. Over the period of years, I failed to see him as a father figure. Instead,

I saw him as a bully and a tyrant. Looking at my life today I can clearly see that this has had a very powerful impact.

Recently, I was in a classroom setting with a man who stood a head taller than myself and who had a gruff voice and manner about him. One day, this man disagreed with a comment I made and became very verbal about it. We had a major argument about it, during which I made it clear that he was nothing more than a coward and a bully.

It was not until later when I was calmer that I realized that when I had been arguing with the man, it was not him I was seeing. Instead, for the time of the argument I was once again a small child being bullied by an adult. In this case however, the small child had enough adult strength and size that he refused to be bullied!

Never let anybody think that one's past does not influence our present. The past has a tremendous impact on the present. Just ask the therapist who treats my post-traumatic stress disorder!

I will not say that my father was a bad man. He became one of the best people a person could know. In fact, I called him a few years before his death and thanked him for putting a foot up my backside when I was young. It shaped me and made a man out of me. However, there were times when he was outright abusive when drinking. Those times were painful, and the scars still exist today.

Serving

I have found that the key to being blessed in life is generosity. It does not matter what walk of life you come from nor what your religion may be. If you are generous, you will find that you are blessed. I am a Christian and my beliefs are based on the Holy Bible so I will probably rely on it for my arguments. However, there are lots of religions where generosity is encouraged because generosity is a basic truth. Truth is universal and of course it is going to make its way into religions. It makes no difference if a person is atheist, Christian, Muslim, Hindu, Wiccan, Animist, or whatever. Truth is universal and love is a universal truth. All religions (or non-religions) know that the benefits of forgiving others far outweigh any benefits one might receive from carrying a grudge. As a future therapist, I have studied the human mind. I know that my biggest task in the future will be to help any clients who cross my path deal with the hurt from their past. As humans, we think it is okay to carry grudges. What we do not realize is that carrying a grudge is like loading a bag full of bricks and dragging it everywhere we go. The bricks may be small, or they may be heavy, but we carry them everywhere we go. We take them to bed with us and carry them all day long. The more grudges we have, the heavier our load becomes. Finally, we get little else done but nursing our grudges. Who wants to carry a ton behind them all the time? I certainly do not! I spent a large portion of my life carrying grudges. I became addicted to drugs as a result and was addicted for years. I finally got clean in a 12-step program that I no longer attend. One of the 12 steps required me to honestly write down all my grudges and identify the emotion behind those grudges. I thought the emotion was anger but much to my surprise I realized the emotion was fear. When I dealt with my fear, I was able to let go of my grudges and forgive those who had harmed me. I realized most of all that I had harmed myself more by carrying those grudges than I had harmed those who hurt me. My grudges do not harm them in the slightest. They go about their lives never giving me a second thought while I am consumed with rage about them! It was senseless on my part. In the end, I had helped them in hurting me by extending their harm far beyond what they intended!

The 12-step program also taught me that if I wanted to stay clean, I had to pull my head out of my behind and start serving others. It taught me essentially that there was a God, and I was not God. For the atheist, it taught me that the world did not revolve around me. I was a mighty small fish in a mighty huge ocean. It taught me that the only path to healing was through service. I began to do little things to help others. At first, my service work was merely cleaning ashtrays after the 12-step meetings. However, I found that even that simple act gave me a sense of purpose. It felt good. I went on to serve the program in many ways, even serving as the regional secretary. In all these things, I found that pulling my head out of my behind and helping others left me feeling useful and blessed. Most of all it helped me quit thinking about the harm others had done to me. That was a gift. I was in the 12-step program for about five years and served in many positions. Then one night, I was walking home from a meeting and walked past a church. The church was holding a service, so I decided to go in. I listened to the preacher as he essentially told my story. Then he gave an invitation. I got up with every intention of leaving. I was sitting at the end of the pew in the very last row so all I had to do was turn left and leave. I stood up, turned right, and went up to the preacher, confessing that he had told my story, and asking him to baptize me. I cannot explain what happened, but I know it changed me. I wanted to do even more service than I had been doing so I left that church and became a soldier in the Salvation Army, where I have tons of opportunities to serve. Service gets me out of myself. The days I do not serve others are now my worst days. When I serve, I do not expect even a thank you because I get more out of it than the one receiving. It is a blessing to give of oneself.

Heartbreak

2016 has been a miserable year. 2014 and 2015 were also terrible years. Each year on New Year's Eve, I would make myself the same promises that the next year would be better. In some ways, the following year would be an improvement. In other ways, it was worse. For example, 2016 is the first year since 2013 that I have not ended the year grieving the death of somebody close to me. In September of 2014, I lost my wife. In February 2015, my father died and then my mother followed in August of 2015. So, 2017 will be the first year I have not started with a broken heart.

My best way of dealing with the past few New Year's Eves has been to attend recovery celebrations. I have been in recovery from long term addiction for almost eight years. If I make it until February 9, 2017, I will celebrate eight years of drug free living. So, unlike many people, going out and getting hammered on New Year's Eve is not an option for me. Therefore, I try to find activities that I can do with no mind-altering substances involved. I have gone to church a few times and celebrated the incoming year with other Christians. My most meaningful way of celebrating it though is to attend functions sponsored by different recovery groups. The traditions of those groups forbid me to name them as the 11th tradition states that members should remain anonymous at the level of press, radio, and film. Many of us have come to include the world wide web as part of that. Therefore, I will not name the groups I attend but will say that I am in recovery.

Recovery parties are always wonderful to me. They are opportunities to do things without mind altering chemicals that I have not done in years. For example, I attended one party and we had a DJ there. We held our meeting as usual and then began dancing and mingling. Somebody talked me into dancing. Now you must bear in mind that I seldom danced even when I was in active addiction. So, I went out on the floor and joined the fun. While I honestly had no idea what I was doing, I mimicked others around me. To my total surprise I won a prize for my dancing! To be honest, I think the judges probably awarded it because I made them laugh. I am certain I looked like a beached whale or a seizure patient flopping around out there! It was fun though and that is what counted most.

New Year's Eve parties are always a welcome relief to me. I am always glad to see the old year go out. It seems that most of the time, all the years bring is hardship so each new one has the glimmer of hope that it may be different. Of course, they never are because life is life. Life is neither fair nor unfair. It is simply life. However, my reactions to life are up to me. I can cry about how unfair life is to me, or I can accept the things about it that are unchangeable and change the rest. Life requires a lot of work. All in all though, it is still good to have those few hours before midnight on January 1 to tell myself that the upcoming year will be easier. If nothing else, it is a mini vacation!

TRUE STORIES

Hot Shot

One September day in my teens, I was out squirrel hunting. I did not particularly get a big thrill out of killing a squirrel, but when you are a member of a big family, you get food wherever you can obtain it.

One day, I came upon a scene that sent chills down my spine and fired anger into my brain. A man who ran a local logging company used horses to pull his logs out of the woods. Many small business owners were simply too poor to afford equipment and horses were much cheaper than bulldozers or other equipment. So, I did not object to them working the horses. What I did object to however was abusing the horses. Apparently, the horses had not performed up to his satisfaction that day and he was trying to force them to perform better. Therefore, he was using a device that I never did believe in and never will use. He was using a cattle prod, also known as a "hot shot". It is a device that you press against the animal and squeeze a trigger, releasing a strong electrical shock. He was repeatedly using the hot shot on first one horse and then the other as his brother held the horses in place by their bridles.

The worst part was that a third person, the son of one of the two men, was dumping buckets of water over the team, making sure the electric shock would have good conduction. They were standing in the middle of a creek doing all of this. Well, I am not one who believes violence ever solve anything, but this scene made my very blood boil and my skin crawl. To say I was livid would be a gross understatement. I had a nuclear meltdown that made Three Mile Island look like a tea kettle boiling over. So, I decided it was time to teach these idiots a lesson.

I spoke up, letting them know I was there as I stepped out of the brush. Then I asked them what on Earth they thought they were doing? They foreman said, "These horses are useless today so we're putting a little fire into them."

"You're putting fire into them by torturing them. Is that it?" I asked.

"No," said Tom, the foreman. "Tom and I have handled our horses this way for years. The hot shot does not hurt them. It only mildly shocks them and puts some spirit into them."

"I'm aware of your hot shots," I replied. "They actually disperse a charge of 120 volts. So, I will tell you what I want you to do. I want you to lay your hot shot on the bank there and roll around in the water getting yourselves good and wet. Then I want you to use the hot shot on each other four times each, rolling around in the water again before each shot."

"And how are you going to make us do that?" Tim, the foreman's brother asked.

"Well, if you don't do it, you're going to have severe lead poisoning," I answered as I cocked and raised my shotgun, pointing it at them.

"You won't do that," Little Tom, the foreman's son stated.

"Are you willing to call my bluff?" I asked. "If you are, I'll shoot you and call the coroner myself. They will probably pin a medal on me anyway."

"I hate to say it," the foreman said as he knelt down into the water, "but I know this kid and he is as crazy as a loon. If he says he will shoot, you can bet he plans to shoot. I also know that he is an expert sharpshooter and will not miss. I'll take my chances with the hot shot!"

"The hot shot will electrocute us," Tim exclaimed. "My God it could kill us!"

"It might," I said. "However, I'm carrying a Remington 12-gauge three-inch magnum pump with seven rounds in it. I am standing 15 feet away on a steep bank above you. From here, it would be like shooting ducks in a pond and I guarantee you this magnum will blow a hole through you that your horses could walk through. So, the hot shot is your only hope. And by the way, I am also taking your horses, tack, and all. My dad will pay you for them."

Tom rolled around in the water and then stood up, asking Tim to shock him with the hot shot. "I can't," Tim said.

"My God," Tom answered. "You don't have a choice. He'll kill us if we don't."

Tim used the hot shot on Tom as commanded and Tom screamed as the shock hit him.

"How does that feel," I asked. "Did you like it? Well neither does your team! Now Tim you lay in the water and take your medicine. Little Tom, I'll let you off the hook because you're only following the orders of these two bullies."

I didn't force any of them to take more than one shock because I wasn't as cruel as they were. I simply wanted to punish them and telling them I was going to force them to administer more than one shock was part of my tactic. After the two brothers had completed their shocking task, I forced them to smash the hot shot with a sledgehammer and send the team of horses up over the hill to me. The horses gladly climbed the bank and I caught one of them at the top. Since the tack was a double tack, catching one caught them both.

"Tell your dad I want $500.00 each for them horses," Tom called out.

"They're worth about $200.00 each," I answered. "I'll ask him to give you $500.00 total."

I took the horses to my house, which was about four miles away. I rode one of them most of the way and it went on to become my pony. Of course, my parents were shocked when I rode up with a team of horses and even more flabbergasted when I told them where the horses came from. My dad nearly had a coronary when I told him I had spoken in his behalf and bought the team, tack, and all for $500.00. However, under the circumstances he said I had done the right thing. My parents were initially concerned that the brothers would have me arrested for assault or something for forcing them to use the hot shot on each other. However, they also doubted that part of my story, though they knew the brothers in question had a reputation for being cruel to horses. My story was confirmed later however when my uncle called. Apparently, one of the brothers had complained to him about my behavior. My uncle had told them to count themselves fortunate because I could have shot them. If I did not, my cousin who was hunting nearby and witnessed the whole incident could have! My uncle also told them they were more than welcome to use his phone to call the sheriff if they wished and the sheriff would arrest me. However, my cousin and I would both testify that they had been mistreating their horses and they would be in the same cell I was but for much longer! Therefore, my parents breathed a deep sigh of relief. "You did the right thing by protecting the horses," my dad told me. “However, I hope you realize it’s going to take me several months to pay for them. I will be paying for them with your allowance. And son, the next time you want to bring an animal home, do us all a favor. Find a stray dog or rescue a bag of drowning kittens!”

Dementia

"Do you see them up there?" my grandfather asked.

"See who Grandpa?" I asked him, turning to look in the direction he was pointing.

"Those Indians," he replied becoming quite animated.

"No Grandpa," I replied. "I don't see them."

"Well, I promise you they're there," he answered. "If we're very quiet, they'll pass by and not notice us."

Thinking it a little strange but knowing nothing about dementia, I went inside and mentioned it to my mother. She told me that he had been watching "Indians" that nobody else could see for several hours. He said they would appear and then disappear again. What we did not realize at the time was that dementia patients often see things that have occurred in their past. My grandfather had been born in 1906. The city in which he lived had been home to many Native Americans, who like everybody else, were trying to scratch out a living.

The occurrences of the native Americans would go on for months. Then winter would set in and he would not be on the porch where he could watch them. Our first real dose of the dangers he was facing would come one night in mid-winter. It had been snowing all day and the air temperature was burr below zero. I was in my bed upstairs when a blast of cold air woke me up. It was typical of our door to blow open if the wind blew hard enough. We seldom ever locked it because it was an era when people could sleep with their doors open. Besides, we were so poor we knew we did not have anything worth stealing anyway. So, I went downstairs to close the door, figuring I would go ahead and lock it while I was at it.

When I got downstairs, I found the door standing wide open and snow blowing into the house. I also noticed that my grandfather was gone. I knew he was not in the bathroom because it was standing open. I immediately knew he had taken off into the night! He had been acting quite strange of late. I awoke my mother and the rest of the family. My father as usual was passed out and there was no waking him. The rest of us, armed with flashlights and anything else we could find to disperse darkness waded into the snow to find our grandfather. Fortunately, I had awakened shortly after he left so even in the falling snow, we easily found his tracks. We followed them to our neighbor's house. Our neighbor had seen us coming. He was standing on his porch when we approached. "Lost something?" he asked. "He wandered up onto my porch about fifteen minutes ago. He was cold so I took him inside and warmed him up. He is drinking some cocoa right now. I figured he came from your house since you are the only new people in the area. I had never met him before tonight. I was going to let him warm up some more and then bring him home."

The incident with the neighbor began a routine of having somebody on constant vigil with him. The somebody was usually me. I became his primary caregiver for the remainder of the time he was in our home. At one point, he was coherent enough to talk to my mother. He made her promise that no matter what happened we would never place him in a nursing home. She and I both promised him we would never allow that to happen.

His condition continued to deteriorate. Finally, he was bed ridden. Most of the time, I was forced to use restraints to keep him in bed. It killed me to restrain him, but I knew it was necessary to prevent him from falling and getting hurt even worse. The medical supply company had supplied us with restraints for him. The restraints allowed him to move his arms but would not allow him to reach the other arm to take the restraints off. However, the restraints came at a high price. I was not a nurse, so I was untrained in preventing pressure sores also known as bed sores. He developed a huge one on his right hip. Surgery was required to correct it. When the surgery was completed, the doctor called the family into a conference. He told us that my grandfather needed more care than we could provide. He said we would have to sign the papers for admission into a nursing home. Failure to do so would result in the state doing it anyway. Mom and I were devastated. What made it even worse was the look on my grandfather's face as some recognition of where he was destined entered the fog that dementia had left behind. My grandfather died two weeks after his admission into the nursing home. Thirty years later, my father died of dementia as well. It is thought that dementia is a genetic disorder. If nothing else takes you out before its onset, dementia will kill the members of succeeding generations. Does that mean I will also die of the disease? More than likely it does. Dementia I hate you!

CHRISTIAN ESSAYS

Thank God

The Holy Bible tells a story in Luke 17: 11-17. In this story, Jesus heals ten men who have leprosy. Now, leprosy may not seem like that big of a deal to us who live in an age where leprosy is curable, but 2,000 years ago, leprosy was serious. A leper was always an outcast because God told the priests to separate the lepers from the rest of the community to prevent the spread of the disease. Sure, God could have cured the lepers, but God chose not to do so. Instead, He ordered the isolated. They would have to walk all by themselves or with other lepers and shout "Unclean" to anybody they encountered. It was not a happy lifestyle.

One day, Jesus encountered ten lepers. Whether the lepers sought him out or not is unclear. It is likely that they did. What is clear is that they asked Jesus to heal them. He did and told them to go and show themselves to the priests. Lepers who no longer had leprosy were required to show themselves to the priest who would announce them cured and make a sacrifice in their behalf. So, the ten headed off toward the priest as instructed and on the way their leprosy was cured. One of the ten stopped and returned to Jesus, thanking Him for curing Him and praising God for his cure.

I am not saying that the other nine were ungrateful. They were cured as well and probably went to the priests as required and were pronounced clean. However, the foreigner among the ten recognized Jesus for who He truly was. Why go to a priest to offer a thank you sacrifice to God when you could walk directly up to God Himself and offer a sacrifice of praise? This was exactly what the tenth leper did! I am not saying he did not eventually go and offer the sacrifice as the law required. He may have. The fact that he was not a Jew may have prevented him from doing so, however. What remains though is that of the ten men cured, only one recognized Jesus as the Messiah and Son of God.

How often do we not say thank you? If I even wake up in the morning, I am thankful! So many times, we focus on what is wrong. Isn't it time to focus on what is right? If we make a list of all that is right in our lives, we will find our problems diminish in comparison! Be thankful!

Doubts

William Shakespeare said, "Our doubts are traitors, and make us lose the good we oft might win, by fearing to attempt."

I am one who also has a lot of self-doubt. I have come to realize however that for me personally, there is a cure for my doubt. I find comfort in my faith in Jesus Christ. While I may turn the judges of the Writer's Cramp off by saying that, particularly if they are not Christian, I am merely expressing how I personally deal with doubt. My way may not work for everybody and that is perfectly acceptable. The God I serve does not go around twisting anybody's arm saying, "Believe in me or I will do this, this, or that."

He does want us to serve Him, but He will not force anybody to do so against their will. I dealt with a lot of doubt early in my Christian faith and found that it often stopped me from taking chances I should have taken. One area where I suffered much doubt was believing that my life was too much of a wreck for me to witness for my Lord. I thought I had to be as pure as the driven snow before I could even begin to let anybody know I was a Christian. I often beat myself over the head with my doubt. I would be talking to somebody that I knew was hungry for the Lord. Their need was really palpable, but I would keep my mouth shut for fear they would see right through me and know that I was just as guilty of wrongdoing as they were. I finally came to realize that we are all sinners if we are in this flesh. We are human, and to be human means to be a sinner. The only person who was ever perfect was Jesus and we murdered Him for it! One day, I was reading the book of Galatians, which is one of the New Testament epistles. In it, I found a scripture in which the Apostle Paul said he had confronted the Apostle Peter because Peter had committed a sinful act, which brought disgrace upon the church. I realized then that even the Apostles, who wrote most of the New Testament, were merely sinners saved by grace. I no longer worry about making Jesus look like a fool by acknowledging that a sinner like me serves Him. I do my best not to screw up, but I make mistakes every day. When I do, I merely ask my Father to forgive me, try not to make the same mistakes, and move forward. Doubt? Yes, I still have doubt, but I find comfort in scripture and know that I am merely human. I'm a sinner saved by grace.

One scripture I get great comfort from is Romans 12:2 which says, "Do not conform to the pattern of this world but be transformed by the renewing of your mind. Then you will be able to test and approve God's will - his good, pleasing, and perfect will."

When I renew my mind through prayer and Bible study, I find that I don't have as many nagging doubts. When I do have doubts, the Spirit of God urges me to go ahead and proclaim the gospel and to allow Him to worry about whether I stumble and look foolish. The world stands ready to judge because the world has this mistaken belief that Christians are to be perfect and sinless. If I allow the world's mistaken beliefs to stop me from proclaiming the gospel, I allow Satan to win. Peter tells us that Satan, "...prowls like a roaring lion seeking somebody to devour."

I stay vigilant by grounding myself with prayer and Bible study.

Eyes on the Prize

We all have trials and troubles in life. So how is it that some people can get through distressing situations totally unscathed? I cannot and will not speak for everybody, but I know what works for me. What works for me is not to take my eyes off Jesus.

When I go to looking at the world instead of Jesus, I get caught up in all the mess and soon, I am part of it. The Apostle Peter gives us a good metaphor for what happens when we take our eyes off Jesus. We read:

> *"Between three and six o'clock in the morning, Jesus came to the disciples, walking on the water. When they saw Him walking on the water, they were terrified. 'It's a ghost,' they said, and screamed with fear.*
>
> *Jesus spoke to them at once, 'Courage!' he said, 'It is I. Don't be afraid.'*

Then Peter spoke up, 'Lord, if it is really you, order me to come out on the water to you.'

'Come!' answered Jesus. So, Peter got out of the boat and started walking on the water to Jesus. But when he noticed the strong wind, he was afraid and started to sink down in the water. 'Save me, Lord!' he cried."

– Matthew 14:26-30

When we take our eyes off Jesus, we have to depend on ourselves. If we could do it, Jesus would not have suffered the horrible death He suffered. The Apostle Paul wrote, *"I have the strength to face all conditions by the power that Christ gives me,"* Philippians 4:13.

Jesus gives us all that same power. All we must do is keep our eyes on Him.

Evolution

Before I go into why I believe that science has consistently proven evolution false, I want to address evolution for exactly what it is: a theory. Newton's three laws of physics are quantifiable, provable facts. They are not assumptions and every experiment that is done regarding them consistently proves them to be true. Newton proved them in his lifetime and the science of even his time could not deny the fact that they were true. They were true then and they remain true today. They were derived from and based on observable facts.

Theories on the other hand are not laws. They are merely guesses based on conjecture. I have a theory that I am going to be a famous writer someday. Does that mean I am a famous writer? No, it does not! It means I think I may become one. The same hold true for the theory of evolution. Scientists talk about evolution as if it were a scientific fact when it is not. It is merely a scientific theory to explain what scientists feel they cannot explain otherwise. It was a theory 150 plus years ago when Charles Darwin presented it and it remains a theory today. Theories are not scientific laws. I can present a theory that 2+2=5 but that does not make my theory true. It is merely my theory.

Now, let us examine evolution a little more deeply. I would begin by asking if Sir Isaac Newton took 150 years to prove his scientific laws to be true? No, he did not! In fact, he lived a grand total of 84 years. Given the fact he would have spent at least 15 of those years simply growing into adulthood, we can assume he theorized and proved his laws to be true within the span of probably fifty years. Yet Darwin presented the theory of evolution 150 years ago and science, which has much better technology than Newton had available, still has not proven evolution to be true. Science can indeed show how a species changes over a period to adapt to its environment, but there is no supporting evidence that any species ever became a different species. Wolves of 5,000 years or even 10,000 years ago may have been the forerunner for the modern dog but there is no supporting evidence that a wolf ever stood on its hind legs and began walking upright as a chimpanzee. In fact, there is no supporting evidence that any creature ever did anything more than changed in whatever ways were necessary to survive in the environment in which it existed. If evolution were true, there would be some fossil evidence of it and there is none. Personally, I would be insulted if there was because I have more respect for myself than to believe any of my ancestors ever swung by their tails from trees. I do not care how far removed they were!

So, what about these so-called prehistoric men? One such was the Piltdown Man. This so-called missing link was found to be a hoax when it was confirmed that the scientists involved in its "discovery" had intentionally combined the skull of an orangutan with a small, brained human.

Nebraska Man was another scientific fraud in which a pig's tooth was passed off as a human tooth. Evolutionists drew pictures of what they believed this creature looked like and they are often used in textbooks today even though they have been proven to be a hoax. Come on people!

Java Man came about because a partial skull bone belonging to an ape was discovered. Sometime later, a clearly human thigh bone was found forty feet way. The scientist doing the digging was so desperate to prove evolution that he assumed the two belonged together. Somebody please tell me that if I were ever buried and a horse was buried 20 feet away, some scientist in 3000 years is not going to excavate me and the horse and claim he has proof centaurs really existed!

Neanderthal Man was another huge hoax. For one thing, the scientist who "discovered" Neanderthal man was forced to resign in disgrace after it was discovered that he had plagiarized the work of his colleague. Thus, anything that had ever come about because of his career became questionable. Secondly, a German scientist confirmed that the skeletal remains the scientist had initially claimed were the "missing link" may have looked like the missing link due to deformities brought on by rickets and osteoporosis but was indeed totally human. However, like the others, Neanderthal Man is still taught as scientific fact in schools. The only thing factual is that it is a hoax.

There have been other 'discoveries' made claiming to be supportive of evolution but when the facts come out, they are either frauds or present insufficient evidence to prove what they truly are.

Evolution as a theory is just that: a theory.

Thermodynamics

I have been discussing the reasons I believe that God is not only real but that He revealed Himself to man through the person of Jesus Christ. So far, I have discussed scientific evidence that proves conclusively that the star of David, also known as the Christmas star, was indeed an actual event. I have shown scientific evidence which proved that carbon dating cannot be used to prove anything that is any older than 11,460 years old. In today's lesson, I am going to present two laws of physics that prove conclusively that the big bang was impossible. The first of those laws is the First Law of Thermodynamics. This law proves conclusively that energy cannot be created or destroyed in an isolated system. In other words, something cannot simply appear out of nothing.

Sir Thomas Aquinas stated that this would be known as the first cause principle. In his five proofs for the existence of God, which we will eventually discuss, the fifth of them is the First Cause. In this argument, he reasons that there had to be something to set everything, life as we know it, in motion. The first law of thermodynamics would agree with him because it clearly states that, "Energy cannot be created or destroyed in an isolated system."

Thus, the idea that the universe suddenly exploded into existence out of nothingness is ludicrous. Something had to be a static or constant which caused the universe as we know it to exist. In other words, something with the capability of creating the universe as we know it had to always exist. The word of God tells us what that something is when it says "Ever since God created the world, his invisible qualities, both His eternal power and His divine nature, have been clearly seen; they are perceived in things that God has made. So those people have no excuse at all," Romans 1:20.

And "God has always been your defense; His eternal arms are your support. He drove out your enemies as you advanced and told you to destroy them all."

Sir Thomas Aquinas states that it is logical to assume the existence of God and illogical to deny it. Would it be logical to say, "I want a new television set," and expect one to just appear out of nothing on one's television stand? No, it would not. Nor is it logical to assume that the universe simply exploded into being out of nothing. Something had to always exist. As the second law of thermodynamics will prove, that something had to be God.

The second law of thermodynamics is that the entropy of a system always increases. In other words, everything that exists is in a constant state of decay. Thus, matter, energy, nor even time itself could have been eternal up to this point. If matter had been eternal as predicted by the big bang theory, then the second law of thermodynamics is not true. The second law of thermodynamics has been proven to be true countless times. Our very existence proves it true. No human being has ever lived forever or existed from eternity. We are born and, barring not dying from an accident, we die of old age or basically because of entropy. Therefore, the theory that the universe was once a huge collection of energy and matter that exploded and by a very lucky roll of the dice formed our planet, our solar system, and likely countless other planets in countless other solar systems is impossible. Matter and energy would have decayed and become nothing long before the big bang could have taken place. The only way the universe could have come into existence is by the intervention of something that is not subject to the laws of thermodynamics. That something would be the God who put the laws of thermodynamics in place to begin with. Sir Thomas Aquinas again calls this the "Argument from Design".

In this argument, Aquinas states that there is order in nature. Since nature itself lacks specific intelligence, something had to put the order in nature. For example, the words I am typing here have a specific order. While I am human and may make an occasional typo, the words are laid out in some logical fashion. They show design. Nature shows design. The laws of thermodynamics show design.

Stay tuned. I am nowhere near done with presenting my reasons for believing that God exists. Science has a lot more to say about the subject.

Carbon-14 Dating

Decaying animals can be used as a sort of clock. The belief is nitrogen molecules in the atmosphere are bombarded by cosmic rays, which then tear the molecules apart. The result is a radioactive form of carbon known as Carbon-14. Carbon in all forms is absorbed by plants, though more Carbon-12 is absorbed than Carbon-14. These plants are then consumed in animals or the animals that eat the plants are consumed by other animals and the Carbon-14 then becomes a part of their makeup. All animals inhale and exhale carbon. However, when they die, they are no longer breathing, thus they have no remaining Carbon-12 to emit. Any carbon coming from them at this point is Carbon-14.

Scientist would have us believe that the amount of this carbon left in decaying objects can thus be measured and dates back millions, even billions of years. However, this simply is not true. Any radioactive product has a rate of decay, which can indeed be tracked. The rate of decay of a radioactive product is known as its half-life. The half-life of Carbon-14 is 5,730 years, meaning that if a decaying object has any Carbon-14 left in it at all, the object can be no more than 11,460 years old. If anything, Carbon-14 dating proves the accuracy of the Bible because everything man has found from coal to oil can be carbon dated. Thus, it can be no older than 11,460 years, which correlates to the Bible's claim that the Earth is approximately 10,000 years old. Given the fact that men often lived to be over 950 years old just after creation, and given the fact that we do not know how long Adam tended the Garden of Eden before he sinned and began dying, 11,640 years is very reasonable.

Another form of dating is by using the decays of other isotopes, which are alleged to be much longer. For example, scientists calculate the rate of decay of say uranium in a rock to determine that it is so many millions of years old because uranium decays very slowly. This decay rate of radioactive isotopes makes scientists think that the earth is millions of years old instead of the ten or so thousand years referenced by God's word. The Christian answer to that is simple. God made all those things and created them to look millions or billions of years old to fool people who were ignorant enough to say the Bible is wrong. God does not lie! Numbers 23:19 and other verses make this clear. We must believe His word and take it at face value.

Wings on Prayers

Many of us have prayed and asked God to do things for us. Often, we expect them to happen instantly and miraculously, but God does not necessarily work that way. He will work a miracle if it is in His will to do so and if there is no human method of getting the job done but sometimes, he expects us to step out on faith. James discusses how faith works when he says, "My friends, what good is it for one of you to say that you have faith if your actions do not prove it? Can that faith save you? Suppose there are brothers or sisters who need clothes and do not have enough to eat. What good is there in saying to them, "God bless you! Keep warm and eat well!" - if you don't give them the necessities of life? So it is with faith, if it is alone and includes no actions, then it is dead," James 2:14-17.

Often, when we are praying for things, we miss out on getting them because we expect God to simply dump them in our laps. Jesus said, "I assure you that if you have faith as big as a mustard seed, you could say to this hill, 'Go from here to there!' and it will go. You could do anything," Matthew 17:20.

What Jesus did not say was that these things would happen if we were willing to put some effort into helping them happen. God wants us to be involved in things. If we need money to pay for an item that we want badly, then God will provide the money. However, it may be in small portions that we are expected to save. God will deposit the money, but we must write the checks!

I like the illustration I heard once. A man was caught in a flood and managed to get to a tree. He climbed up in the tree and prayed that God would save him. In a while, somebody came by in a rowboat and asked him to get in. He refused. He stated that God would save him. Next, a bass boat came by and he again refused to go with them. At last, a helicopter came by and dropped a rescue harness. Again, he refused because God would save him. So, he drowned. He asked God why God had not saved him, and God said, "I sent a rowboat, a bass boat, and a helicopter. You refused my help."

Folks, God is willing to help those who are willing to help themselves. We must do things His way and within his will.

POETRY

Limericks

St. Patrick's Day

I dearly love St. Patick's Day
I would have it no other way
My shamrock and I
Oh what a great guy
St. Patrick's green is on display!

Old Woman from Norse

There was an old lady from Norse
Who wanted to purchase a young horse
Her husband told her no
She bought the horse though
She was hurt when it bucked of course!

Pub Closed!

St. Patrick's Day and pubs were closed
Due to Corona she supposed
She could have no ale
Her brain would now fail
Patrick for one was opposed!

Chili

There was a woman from Philly
Whose man wanted a pot of chili
She said, "Now don't even start
It makes old foul, stinky farts"
Yet she cooked it there in Philly!

Billy Goats

The troll hurt a billy goat gruff
The troll thought he was bad and tough
Then he met big brother
He then feared the other
He was so scared he lost his stuff!

Triolet Poetry

Froot Loops

Froot Loops are my favorite food
I eat them by the box
I love them in any mood
Froot Loops are my favorite food
To eat them I am sneaky like a fox
I eat them if they were as hard as rocks
Froot Loops are my favorite food
I eat them by the box!

Christmas is on the Way

The ham is in the oven
Christmas is on the way
Santa is really shovin'
The ham is in the oven
Witches are dancing in their coven
Soon it will be Christmas day
The ham is in the oven
Christmas is on the way.

Sonnets

Dinner for Two

Married 33 years ago this year
She is still beautiful to him
In her heart he is always near
Only death could separate them.

Dinner at a diner all this time
Each year on this their wedding day
Tonight something with the spoon's chime
The necklace bought from the display.

She says then that he should not have
Though she knows it is not quite true
She is the wife that he should have
It is the least that he can do.

Married now for all these short years
Nineteen Eighty Four calms all fears.

Broken Heart

My broken heart yearns for you
That just seems to be all I do
You left me so long ago now
You would think I would move on somehow.
I tell you I love you every day
Your memory never seems to go away
I will never forget seeing you depart
Your passing literally broke my heart.
I guess I will always see you in my mind
True love is indeed hard to find
I am so glad you were my wife
I wish you were still in my life.
They say parting is sweet sorrow
I dream we will always have tomorrow.

Loving You

As I walk the city street
I see the sights and hear the sounds
Where us two legged creatures meet
I love you so much my heart pounds.
Our love is snow white and pure
It will always stay true
For my loneliness you are the cure
You lifted me when I was blue
I have faced the black of night
I have held you in my dreams
I hold you there so tight
We stand and face the daybreak beams.
Us humans are meant to love
You are a gift from God above.

My Lord and King

You are my Lord, my God, and only King
You paid the price to save my worthless soul
For my God I would not refuse anything
You died horribly to make me whole.
You left heaven to bear a rugged cross
You did not hesitate to come to earth
You did not once consider it a loss
You came to us by way of virgin birth.
You lived here for years a carpenter's son
You labored through your life so long and hard
From the cross you did not try to run
Both your hands and feet are totally nail scarred.
You will forever be my Lord and my God
I will never begin to find that odd.

My True Love

There are no words that will tell you how I love you
My love is not something I can express in words
You are the world to me and I do so love you
We are to be somehow joined as two great love birds.
When I look in your eyes a light is there so bright
May my soul now put out the fire I have inside
You can make my life on this Earth feel long and right
Inside I am on fire with love no one can hide.
May I put my rope on your heart this day on out
No one can stop the way this heart has now thus fell
Somehow inside we have much life to go no doubt
Without you I would not go on with life do tell.
May I somehow express love that is now complete
No one has loved like you so full, so true, so sweet.

Son of God

Each year we celebrate His birth
The King of Heaven and Lord of Earth
God knew man was in dire straits
He sent His Son to pay sin's rates.
Jesus, not known by all
Some refuse to hear His call
Many will die never calling His name
They have only their self to blame.
Jesus was and is alive
He came that we might all survive
To Him He wants us to cling
Not just His praises sing.
Come one and all to the cross
Then your soul suffers no loss.

We Three Kings

We were kings who wandered from afar
We were in search of the promised child
We followed the bright and shining star
And found him in a town lowly and mild.
We were kings who had known no lack or want
Yet inside we were lonely and in need
Our love for the chosen one knew no daunt
We knew not that for us he would soon bleed.
A little child laying in a manger
The Savior of the whole human race
A man like which none was ever stranger
A man so full of mercy and of grace.
We were kings who reigned down here below
His kingdom was the one we sought to know.

Snowy Evening

A Snowy Evening in the Deep Woods
The poem that won my heart
I knew reading it that I'd write for good
I knew it from the start.
Robert Frost won me over
Way to write it sir
He made wish on the clover
He left my heart astir.
He died the year I read the poem first
It was in the year 1969
The poem gave me unquenchable thirst
It suited me just fine.
I still love reading Robert Frost
Snowy Evening or Road Less Taken.

ORIENTAL POETRY

Than Bauk Poetry

Birds on a Wire

Birds on a wire
hearts desire to
admire the sight.

Caffeine

I love my tea
and coffee so
give me caffeine.

Hot Coffee

Coffee is not
very hot I
forgot to check.

Teatime

I drink my tea
and then she joins
with me in love.

Summer

Summer is here
time to cheer as
birds clearly chirp.

Storm

Thunderstorm booms
lightning zooms down
in rooms we hide.

Tweets

Their pretty tweet
sounds so sweet and
I greet the sounds.

Haiku

snowy days

much snow on the ground
thus the weather is so cold-
snowman could care less

starfish

starfish laying on
shore used as skipping stones used
children now at play

groundhog

the groundhog hides his
face from the sun except
on groundhog day: yes?

barn

it is just a barn
animals inside locked away
meat coming soon

soothing water

alone in darkness
listening to a flowing stream
calming is the water

fall

the time of falling
leaves is upon us once
more - blazing fires now

Various Oriental Types

police guns

police carry guns
guns kill people
who polices the police

Soul Mates

I am so in love with you
Each day I love you anew
You are the queen of my soul

I wish I could hold you
Right now love will have to do
For you will ever own my soul.

The distance keeps my heart in a brew
I know that we will make it through
You will always match my soul.

Autumn

autumn falling here
West Virginia air cooling
trees turning soon now
as animals prepare for
the gloomy months yet to come

About the Author

Chris Breva was born Marvin D. Schrebe, on June 9, 1961. He was a storyteller from the time he could talk. His mother knew he had a vivid imagination and did not punish him for it. Once he learned to write, he began writing stories and his classmates began to encourage his gift by trading his written stories with each other. Chris always had a gift for words. His fourth grade reading teacher timed his reading abilities and determined that he was reading and comprehending about 400 words per minute. The teacher encouraged his love of words and introduced him to poetry. The first poem Chris read was "*Snowy Evening in the Deep Woods*" by Robert Frost. Chris knew from that moment that he would be a writer.

His parents also knew he would be a writer. His father read one of Chris's stories and took it to his job, where the secretary typed it. Attempts were made to publish the story but by itself it was not enough to publish. Chris would go on to publish four books between 2003 and 2010 as well as self-publishing four others.

Chris is a certified peer recovery support specialist and addictions counselor. He knows the rigors of addiction very well having suffered personally. He now has twelve years of sobriety and works to bring recovery and serenity to others. He is an ordained minister and devout Christian. He serves Jesus Christ on a daily basis and is happy to discuss his faith.

www.ingramcontent.com/pod-product-compliance
Lightning Source LLC
LaVergne TN
LVHW011942070526
838202LV00054B/4766
9781954371866